Turkeys

A Licking Thicket Novel

Lucy Lennox

May Archer

Turkeys

Hunter Jackson's Sage Advice for a Happy Thanksgiving

When your turkey-thieving, town-abandoning, former childhood friend reappears in Licking Thicket after fifteen long years, looking like a snack and smelling like all your favorite treats put together, it might be tempting to, well, *dig in*.

Don't.

And when your plan to teach the man a lesson goes spectacularly awry, becoming less of a wattle-wearing walk of shame around the Thicket's Thanksgiving festival and more of a sexy turkey-twerk in a skin-tight bird costume featuring the hottest pair of drumsticks the town's ever seen, you might think it's time to get over your feud and, well, *take a bite.*

Resist.

But when Charlton Nutter finally shows you the sweet, pure heart he's hiding under all his fine, big-city feathers, and you realize, thanks to the town's meddling matchmakers, that the man is hungry for the kind of love and belonging that only the Thicket can provide, you might decide that both of you have been acting like a pair of turkeys, and in that case you should...

Gobble. Him. Up.

Authors' Note

A few words about Thanksgiving.... and TURKEYS.

Thanksgiving is a big deal in the U.S. The holiday itself is the fourth Thursday of November, but the celebration is a multi-day affair. Most businesses and schools close at midday Wednesday and remain closed through the weekend. (Big thanks to retail and essential workers who don't have this luxury!) The day after Thanksgiving is Black Friday, the unofficial start of the holiday shopping season. And the Sunday after Thanksgiving is the busiest travel day in America.

The Thanksgiving feast features a truly wild array of foods including, but not limited to: mashed potatoes, sweet potato casserole, macaroni and cheese, green bean casserole, ham, collard greens, corn bread stuffing, creamed onions, sausage stuffing, lasagna, various salads, butternut squash, corn pudding, relish, cranberry sauce, bread rolls, pies, crumbles, cobblers, cakes, puddings, and tarts. The foods on each table (and the way they're prepared) are as unique as the people gathered around them, representing each family's particular cultures and traditions. But for most people, the star of the feast is the humble TURKEY (or plant-based turkey substitute), so much so that turkeys are synonymous with this warm and fuzzy holiday.

Which is why it's pretty ironic that *calling* someone a turkey is the opposite of warm and fuzzy. A TURKEY is an exceptionally foolish individual who makes really questionable choices...

And we're not saying that describes Hunter and Charlie at the beginning of this story, but we're not *not* saying it, either.

Happy Reading!
- Lucy & May

Chapter One

Charlton

They say "you can never go home again." Unfortunately, I was learning this was not true. Notably, I felt the concept should be corrected to "you *should* never go home again"... especially if "home" was a tiny speck of southern-fried lunacy somewhere in north-middling Tennessee.

I stared out the front window of the town car at the sign flapping in the breeze above Walnut Street and stifled a groan.

It's Stuffin' Time! the sign proudly proclaimed in bright orange paint, though it was unclear whether this was a threat or a promise. *How many Thicketeers' goodies can YOU fit in your pie hole this Thanksgiving? Stuff your neighbors and get stuffed in return this Wednesday morning. All are welcome! The more the merrier!* At the bottom, a dancing parade of red, brown, and orange handprint turkeys looked way too much like people raising their hands to volunteer as tribute.

"Whoa. So, ah... this is your hometown, huh?" my driver asked. He'd been silent and professional from the moment he'd picked me up at the airport in Nashville, but it was clear his professionalism was no match for the tsunami-level force of the Thicket's pun-tastic holiday cheer.

One could hardly blame him.

"I'm from Chicago," I corrected, silently adding "*now*" to the end of my statement and telling myself it wasn't a lie. "I have family here, but I haven't visited in years."

"Right," he agreed, still staring at the sign like the double entendres might disappear if he looked hard enough. More fool him—nothing much changed in this town, ever, and the puns were eternal. "It's, ah... it's real different here, huh?"

I snorted. *Understatement.*

Licking Thicket—the actual, believe-it-or-not, on-the-map name of the town where I'd grown up—was considered by most folks in the area to have a sort of "rustic charm." A lovely place to live, they said. A welcoming and safe place to raise a family. A fine locale for any human with an affinity for rich soil and hearty livestock. A haven for those who enjoyed seasonal festivals, zany local rituals, and terrible double entendres.

And this was true.

But for those of us who'd had the good sense to leave the place, the Thicket was more rustic than charming and held way too many embarrassing memories to ever be comfortable.

It was not, for example, a place where a man's colorful polos and tasteful but quirky business socks had ever earned him any sort of respect or deference.

Not a place where a gay man could hope to find romance since it was probably the world's only Grindr dead zone.

Definitely not a place where a man could hope to find a decent espresso, let alone an iced, skinny salted-caramel oat milk latte (no whip), either, since the town boasted more dairy cows than humans.

And it was most certainly not a place where people appreciated a heroic (if somewhat misguided) rescue carried out to avert a senseless tragedy.

"Never been out this way," the driver went on. His eyes pinged from side to side as we made our way up the main drag, while I firmly kept my gaze on my phone, but I knew without looking exactly what he was seeing: the ancient "community center," a renovated barn where all the most important Thicket gatherings had been held since the dawn of time; the Feed and Seed with its 1950s vibe; the Thicket Tavern, which was a throwback to the 1970s; the high school with its Fighting Bovines logo that I'd thought was so impressive when I was a child and so scornfully silly once I'd left town for St. Killian's Prep.

"Pretty cool that your town has a bakery that does gluten-free, though," he said cheerfully. "My girlfriend would kill to find a gluten-free place near us. And the Wisteria Cafe says you can 'support local schools with every sip.' What's that about?"

I looked up and frowned at the little clapboard building across from the Tavern. The building itself was old, but the businesses inside it were unfamiliar. After a moment, I shrugged. "Couldn't say. But when I was growing up, the closest thing to a coffee shop in town was the McDonald's out by the highway, so I doubt whatever we'd be *sipping* is anything like we'd be used to in civilization." I picked at a piece of lint on my cuff. "You're from Nashville, right?"

"Nah." The GPS called out a warning, and the driver

took a smooth right turn onto a residential street lined with historical homes. "Grew up in LA, actually. But the scene there is shit for getting discovered, so I moved out here. You listen to country music?"

"Not if I can help it," I said, hoping he wasn't planning to pitch me some kind of demo.

"Well, if you change your mind, me and some friends—"

"Oh, look, almost there," I said, cutting him off before he could beg me to find him at amateur night in some dive bar off-off-*off*-Broadway—which was to say *Nashville* Broadway, the one with more pickup trucks and less Steven Sondheim. "You can pull up by the house with the, ah... green tractor mailbox."

Despite my mood, the familiar John Deere tweaked a long-forgotten thread of sentimentality deep in my chest. My great-grandfather Mortie Nutter had hand-carved the thing as a gift for my uncle when he'd taken over the running of the farm. Every year after that, Uncle Amos had painstakingly cleaned it and touched up the paint to keep it in top condition. It was a symbol of his pride in our family homestead, and it had become an iconic landmark when giving directions to anywhere on this side of the Thicket, even back when I was a kid.

I swallowed. "You can pull over by the barn and that white pickup. Thanks."

Before the town car's tires had crunched to a stop, the front door of the farmhouse opened and out spilled a metric fuck ton of various Nutters and neighbors who still, after all these years, treated the arrival of any newcomer as a rare treat.

My mother's designer pantsuit stuck out like a sore thumb from the assortment of denim and elastic-based cotton knits everyone else sported. I had no idea what expression I was wearing, but when she spied me, she lifted a carefully sculpted eyebrow in maternal challenge through the back window of the car.

I rolled my eyes in response.

Three weeks ago, when she'd browbeaten me into agreeing to spend Thanksgiving in Licking Thicket, my mother had made a snarky comment about my inability to last five days in town without offending anyone. She seemed not to remember that I'd spent the last five years toiling for a boss who made Attila the Hun seem woke and cuddly in comparison and that when I'd been named VP of distribution and logistics last month, there'd been no question that I'd earned the promotion as much for my diplomatic skills as for my understanding of logistics and supply chain management.

So, naturally, I'd done what any man would do when his mother impugns his honor in such a fashion: I'd challenged Katherine Nutter to a nice-off. Whichever of us lasted the longest in Licking Thicket without causing a scene, starting a fight, or creating a mortal enemy would win the prize of their choice—my mother had already told me that she'd be escaping Nashville for a few days to enjoy the Waldorf Chicago's luxury day spa as her prize—as well as bragging rights for eternity.

Unfortunately for her, I was not planning to lose. Not when my reputation was at stake.

I plastered on a grim smile as I thanked my driver and exited the vehicle.

"Uncle Junior, you're here!" someone cried from the middle of the pack. Three kids, including my cousin Jack, came running from around the side of the house, skidding to a stop just before knocking me to the ground.

"I go by Charlton," I corrected, even though I knew

from experience no one would listen. "Sometimes, Charlie—"

"Junior! We ain't seen you in a yonk's age," an adult voice interrupted. The words almost sounded like an accusation, and they instantly made me bristle.

Nice-off, I reminded myself.

I glanced up, smiling even more determinedly, and met my aunt Bell's eyes. "Aunt Bell. Good to see you."

She wrinkled her nose. "What's happening with your face, son? You been in some kind of accident?"

A snorting sound came from the crowd that sounded distinctly like my mother's smug chortle.

"No, ma'am," I said smoothly. "Of course not. I'm just happy to see all y'all!"

I snapped my teeth shut in shock. Where the *fuck* had that come from? Not just "y'all" but "*all* y'all"? Christ, was it that easy to slip back into Southernese? How abhorrent.

Uncle Amos pushed his way through the cluster of people and held his arms out for an embrace. "Well, finally. Bring it on in, Junior. Give us some love, boy."

I let out a breath and felt myself smile for real. "Amos, it's good to see you." I stepped forward and gave him a hug, inhaling his familiar scent—a combination of hay and cows and Charles potato chips—that reminded me of everything I'd loved best about childhood.

After the hug, Amos pulled back and studied me. His gnarled hands clutched my upper arms in a firm grip, proving he was still plenty strong despite the fact he carried a cane these days and was supposedly long retired from running the farm.

"Didja see the sign I left for you?" he demanded.

"The... sign about the Stuffin'?" I was trying very hard not to sound horrified. "That wasn't for me, was it?"

"Nah, I meant the WELCOME, JUNIOR sign. On the cows."

"Oh. No. I was checking my email, and I must've..." I shook my head. "Wait. *On* the cows?"

"Last couple years, Uncle Amos has taken to spelling things out by painting letters on his cows' flanks," my cousin Ollie explained. "You know, the herd he keeps in the far pasture, out by the new Welcome to Licking Thicket sculpture?"

"Trouble is," Ollie's wife Kendra interjected, sounding almost apologetic, "the cows move around an awful lot, and some of 'em even hide in the trees. Joanie Brightly's still angry at Amos over the sign he put out there a few months ago."

"Really? What'd it say?" I wondered.

"Probably best if we don't rehash it." My cousin Frank, the sheriff, rocked back and forth on his booted heels, lips twitching in amusement. "When the letters transpose themselves... let's just say that things get a bit confusing."

I nodded. I was definitely confused.

"Ah, well. It's real good to have you home in any case," Amos said roughly, meeting my eyes and seeming to peer directly into my very soul. Amos was the kind of person who seemed jokey and hokey on the surface but actually saw and felt much more.

I squirmed under his inspection.

"You'll do." He nodded and clapped me on the shoulder once. "And what's more, you'll fetch a high price at the Biddin' tonight," he added proudly.

"The..." I looked around at the assembled Nutters, all of whom seemed to take this pronouncement in stride. "The what now?"

"Oh, that's right. The Biddin' wasn't around when you

lived here, was it?" Kendra mused. "Well, you know how Aunt Angela—"

"Lord rest her soul," Aunt Bell intoned.

"—loved the bachelor auction at the big Lickin' festival every August? The Beautification Corps decided it would be nice to honor her by doing a similar thing for charity every November. We all get involved."

"Sure do. The Biddin' raises money for the Castration Society," Amos said solemnly. "Which I can tell you, after twenty-seven years of marriage, was a cause near and dear to your aunt's heart."

"Uh. Okay?" I blinked. "But I don't—"

Amos clapped me on the shoulder again and turned toward the house. "Wear your Sunday best, and you'll do fine," he called over his shoulder.

I stared after him as if anything he'd said had made a lick of sense—then winced at my own thoughts. *Lick? Really?* Why was it so damn easy to slip back into old habits?

"For the love of Christ," I muttered.

"Don't take the Lord's name in vain, Junior," Aunt Bell snapped. "God Almighty, you'd'a thunk you were raised in a barn." She turned to follow Uncle Amos into the house.

I gaped after her before turning to my mother. "Did she or did she not just take the Lord's—"

"You know the rule around here. 'Do as I say, not as I do.'" Mother patted me on the back.

"Maybe when I was a child, but I'm an adult now. I'm not going to simply go along with whatever cockamamie—"

"I wonder," she interrupted, tapping her lip thoughtfully, "if the Waldorf's spa does those caviar conditioning body wraps I've heard about. They're incredibly expensive, of course, but if someone else was footing the bill..."

I snapped my mouth shut and narrowed my eyes in betrayal. "You put Amos up to this, didn't you? Are you really that determined to win this contest?"

"Charlton Nutter." My mother pressed a hand to the front of her silk blouse, all affronted innocence. "If you'll recall, this 'nice-off' business was your idea. You are my one and only son. I *love* you. Nothing on earth is more important to me than my precious child's happiness. I've only ever wanted what's best for him."

"I know," I admitted grudgingly.

"But if that happens to come with a 24-karat-gold facial and an eight-handed Swedish massage, then so much the better... *Junior*." She pressed a kiss to my cheek and headed after Amos also, leaving a cloud of Opium perfume in her wake. For all of my mother's designer snobbery and couture tastes, she'd never quite escaped the young bride she'd been in the 1980s.

Before I'd fully processed my mother's admission, an older woman with familiar kind eyes and a head of perfectly shellacked curls approached me with her hand extended. "Been a while since we saw one another, so I'm not sure if you remember me. I'm..."

"Emmaline Proud," I said, drawing the name from some hidden recess of my brain.

Her pleased smile was almost girlish. "Amos said you wouldn't forget. You probably heard that he and I got married a little while back? I'm Emmaline Proud Nutter now. No hyphen."

"Of course." I was pretty sure I'd sent a fruit basket or some flowers, and it suddenly occurred to me how very inadequate that was. "Uh... Congratulations."

"Thank you, sweetheart. We didn't do a real big ceremony or anything. You might notice we're not as young as your average newlyweds," she confided.

"Not at all," I lied.

"But we're happy. Amos was my first beau, once upon a time, you see. We weren't right for each other then, but it's funny how time changes folks in some ways and not others." She grinned. "Anyway, I know how busy you are back in Chicago—Amos brags on you and your accomplishments all the time—but it means the world to him that you came to spend Thanksgiving here, Junior. And *that* means the world to *me*."

"Oh." I felt my face heating, both at the idea of Amos "bragging on" me and at her genuine gratitude for me coming back. Suddenly, it was hard to remember exactly why I'd stayed away. "It's not really a big deal."

"It *is*," she insisted. "You know how much family means to Amos, but you in particular have always been special to him. He thinks of you as his own son, especially since—" A shadow crossed her face, and she placed a comforting hand on my arm. "All of us in town were all real sad to hear about your father."

I wondered, for a bewildered moment, if they'd somehow erroneously heard that my father had passed away, rather than the more pathetic truth—that he'd chosen instead to sleep his way across Middle Tennessee before finally being rewarded by falling in love with the grown daughter of an obscenely wealthy country music star. By the time my mother had sued him for spousal and child support, he'd already remarried into a bottomless pit of money.

For years, every time I heard "The Ballad of Whiskey Bend" on the radio, I silently thanked Rusty Jennings for helping get my mom and me out of Licking Thicket.

Because of the Jennings fortune and my father's court-ordered willingness to share it with us, I'd been sent to an elite boarding school in Illinois, which had changed the trajectory of my life.

"Thank you, but my father lives on a fifty-four-acre luxury estate in Franklin," I told her. "He rubs elbows with famous people and eats hundred-dollar bills for brunch. I'm sure he's doing fine." I didn't like my own testy tone, so I tried to mitigate it with a return of my smile. "I appreciate the support, though."

"No need to thank me. What else is family for? Now that I'm Amos's, you're mine," she said, like it was the easiest thing in the world.

Something about the simple statement got to me, and I cleared my throat. "Well. I suppose I should get inside and find out what this 'Biddin' thing is all about, huh?"

Emmaline wrapped her thin arm around my elbow and drew me through the autumn sunshine toward the house. "Oh, you'll find it all very self-explanatory. In fact, it might be best if you don't overthink it," she advised.

But Emmaline had no idea who she was dealing with. Overthinking was my specialty.

Once I'd been shown to my room—the same bunk room with sturdy wooden beds and flannel duvets where I'd had many a "cousin sleepover" back in the day—and dropped off my bag, I immediately headed downstairs to the kitchen. As expected, I found that was where most of the younger members of my family had congregated over coffee and store-bought sugar cookies, while the older folks were probably sitting in the parlor.

"Okay, be real," I said to the group at large, sliding my ass onto a stool by the scarred butcher-block island. "What's this auction thing about? Because Uncle Amos mentioned castration in the same breath that he told me to dress up, and I admit to some concerns."

My cousin Savannah laughed as she fetched a mug from an open shelf and set it in front of me. "It's exactly like Amos explained—a bachelor auction, kinda. Coffee?"

I nodded, and she turned to fetch the pot.

"Not only bachelors anymore, though," her brother Fletcher interjected. "Remember how LaTonya got her wife to volunteer? And Nic did it for three years running, and they wouldn't appreciate being called a bachelor."

There was a lot of information to unpack in this.

"LaTonya's *wife* volunteered to be auctioned off for a date," I repeated. "Along with Nic, who is..."

"Nonbinary." My little cousin Jack cruised into the kitchen, grabbed two cookies, and jammed them both into his mouth without pausing. At my look of confusion, he explained around a spray of cookie crumbs, "Vat means vey don' idennify as a girl o' a boy. Or mebbe as bofe."

"I know what nonbinary means," I said, frowning as Jack ran off again. I just... hadn't been aware that there were nonbinary people living openly in the Thicket or that my ten-year-old cousin would know any.

"Milk?" Savannah held a quart bottle over the mug she'd poured me.

"No. Thank you." I put my hand over the top of the mug. "I, ah, only do oat milk these days." It came out sounding like an apology, and I hated myself for it.

"Sure." Savannah shrugged and returned the bottle to the fridge. "Anyway, the auction used to be called the 'Love on the Lick Castration Fundraiser,' but these days, most of us just call it the Biddin'. And Fletcher's right that it's not a dating or matchmaking thing per se. It's more like buying a few hours of someone's time and attention."

Jaden called from the kitchen table, "That's why LaTonya wanted her wife to volunteer, or so she said. Apparently, Maureen had been promising to sort through their old baby stuff in the garage and bring it to the donation center but kept putting it off. LaTonya won a whole afternoon from her in the auction just so Maureen couldn't wriggle out of the job."

"That's a terrible example," Jaden's twin brother, Jory, said from his place on the sofa in the family room. "Because now LaTonya's waddling around like she swallowed a watermelon seed, and all that baby stuff is back in the nursery waiting for kid number three. I guarantee, whatever those ladies got up to that day, it wasn't cleaning the garage."

Everyone laughed except me. I was still confused. Openly gay, family-having Thicketeers was like a complicated statistics problem; nothing fit into any familiar pattern of what I knew about this place.

"Don't stress, Junior. It's all in good ·fun." Savannah must've caught my wariness and attributed it to nerves because she patted me on the shoulder soothingly. "See, the Castration Society pays for the spay and neuter programs at the local animal shelter, and that ain't cheap, which everyone in town ends up taking their turn on the auction stage at one point or another. Uncle Amos probably thought you'd fetch a high price since so many folks will want the chance to catch up with you."

They would? I wasn't sure about that at all.

"Your definition of *fun* is fucked, Savannah," Fletcher said sourly. "When Amos roped me in last year, I spent a full night playing cribbage for money at the old folks home out on Faulkner Road. I lost forty bucks to Ethel Winalski, and I swear my favorite jacket still smells like Icy Hot."

"Pfft. You got off easy." Jory poked his head over the top of the sofa. "I babysat for Ava Siegel and her fourteen billion children, who all gave me big, sad eyes until I agreed to do Disney karaoke with them, over and over and over again. To this very day, I find myself singing the *Moana* soundtrack in the shower." He shuddered.

"Sure, bro. That's why," Jaden teased, then ducked and laughed when his brother lobbed a couch pillow at him.

"I just don't think you should be able to use your winning bid for evil," Jory insisted stubbornly. "That's all."

Savannah rolled her eyes. "Shush, both of you. It's not always like that. Just think about Willow Norris and Riley Fanning. Willow won a date with Riley, and now the two of them are married and raise boutique livestock."

I wasn't quite sure what that meant, but it was nice to know some winning bids had a happy ending.

I took a deep breath. "So it doesn't matter, then, that I'm, you know... *gay?*"

My sexuality had never exactly been a secret. My mother had probably known before I had, and I recalled a horrifying safe-sex talk with Amos back in high school that began with, "Sometimes, Charlton, when a young bull stud gets real riled over another bull stud..." But I was suddenly very aware that I'd never said the words out loud in this house, in front of these people.

Three sharp gasps came from around the room, and my shoulders instantly stiffened.

"Gay, you say?" My dad's cousin Charli clasped a hand to her chest, but her eyes danced. "My gracious! Why didn't anyone tell me? We coulda found you a nice young man, Junior. Maybe one of the Johnson boys..."

"The happily married Johnson boys?" her husband, Milt, cut in with a grin. "You'd be taking your life in your hands if Cindy Ann heard you say that." To me, he added, "I think what Charli's trying to say is we've known you were gay for a while, kiddo."

I looked around the assembled faces and saw several nods of agreement and not a single flicker of discomfort. For a hot second, I started to wonder if maybe I'd misjudged Licking Thicket in my memories—

"I knew it the day Charli took us to play putt-putt the summer after eighth grade," Fletcher cut in. "You wore that pink golf shirt, remember?" He snickered, and Charli laughed lightly.

Or maybe this town was even worse than I'd recalled. I closed my eyes for a brief moment and reminded myself that I was playing *nice*. "You can't actually determine some-one's sexuality by their clothing, Fletcher."

"Well, of course not." Charli wrinkled her nose. "Fletcher means you spent the first six holes staring at the Jackson boy who was doing the landscaping. When he turned around and caught you, your face turned the same color as your shirt, and you whacked your ball so hard it landed in the bed of Amos's pickup... all the way out in the parking lot. Kind of a dead giveaway if you ask me."

I opened my mouth, then closed it again, feeling my face heat. "Oh. Right. I'd, ah... forgotten that," I admitted. Or possibly I'd blocked it out along with most of my embar-rassing Thicket memories.

Jaden, Jory, and the others laughed out loud.

Savannah shot Charli a glare and patted my shoulder again. "Thanks for trusting us with that all the same, Junior," she said pointedly. "Coming out ain't easy. We can't all be Brooks Johnson, announcing it on stage at the Lickin'."

"Wait," I said, leaning forward. "Brooks Johnson came out?"

"Mmhmm. Dunn Johnson too," Milt agreed. "Apparently, they're all some kinda gay over there."

"Not their sister." Savannah shrugged. "Though Hailey Thompsen was hoping for a while."

Jaden met my eyes. "Anyway, Amos already told the organizers you were gay, Junior. It's in the bio they'll read out while you walk the runway."

"Walk the... Wait, they wrote me a bio?" I asked, voice sliding a little too high in pitch. I could only imagine what any bio of me would include. "What if I don't want to do this?"

My mother swanned into the room at that exact moment and pinned me with a look. "If you don't want to do the auction, that's your choice, Charlton. It would be the *nice* thing to do, of course, but if you're not comfortable, then that's that." She smiled brightly. "You know what *is* comfortable, though? A shiatsu massage and a silk peel facial, especially when paired with a eucalyptus steam shower experience. *Heavenly.*"

I gritted my teeth. "Never mind. I'm doing it."

"You sure?" she asked solicitously.

"Oh, positive. It's every boy's *dream* to be paraded in front of a bunch of Thicketeers like livestock while someone reminds the town of the most mortifying moments of my life in surround sound." I didn't add that this was the sort of dream that one usually woke up from sweating and nauseous. "And then, if I'm very lucky, I'll get to spend a few hours mucking stalls or something? Couldn't be more excited. Really. So glad to be spending the holiday at home."

"Thought so," my mother singsonged before fucking back off to the parlor... or wherever it was she'd come from.

Jory made his way over to the fridge, where he cracked open a beer and took a deep swig. "Don't worry about that either, Junior. Uncle Amos also told the organizers that any date you go on needs to happen ASAP... on account of you never stick around for long."

Whether intentional or not, Jory's words had scored a direct hit. For the first time since I'd arrived, silence fell around the kitchen. My family members looked uncomfortable, and none of them could meet my eyes.

I'd made avoiding trips to the Thicket a perverse kind of sport over the years, and I didn't regret that... mostly. Even when I was a kid, it had been clear there wasn't anything for me in this town—no career opportunities, no romantic prospects, no way to escape being Junior-Nutter-whose-Dad-ran-off... No future.

But sitting here in this ancient kitchen, surrounded by these fuckers who managed to be incredibly annoying and incredibly, weirdly *kind* at the same time, I was starting to remember that there were things I'd liked—*loved*, even—about the Thicket, before I'd started to hate it.

And mostly what I'd loved were the people. My family.

"I'm here now," I reminded Jory and everyone else. "So catch me up on what I've missed, for God's sake. Who were voted Mr. and Ms. Licking Thicket this year? Do y'all still have the parade?"

"Oh, Jesus, now *that* is a story," Savannah said, hopping up onto the counter beside me. "You remember Lurleen Jackson drives that big-ass Buick? *Well...*"

Everyone started talking at once, tripping over themselves to speak, and as I relaxed just enough to let the conversation wash over me, I found myself smiling.

I'd spent a long time trying to make myself into someone new, someone better, than Junior Nutter from the Thicket. But there was something to be said for being *known* too. Being understood. Being cared for.

Maybe it was okay to go home after all, I thought. *At least for a little while.*

But a few hours later, I was singing a different tune.

Chapter Two

Hunter

"Done." I finished securing the last piece of hardware on the rolling door, set the drill next to my toolbox, and turned to the man on the far side of the barn. "*Finally*. Thanks again for helping me knock this out before the long weekend. If I spend the next couple days sanding the edges of the floor and getting it all stained, Alana can get the pictures she needs for the website and start booking spring and summer weddings."

"Anytime. You're family, Hunter, or near enough." Brooks Johnson yanked off his ball cap and ran fingers through his sweaty hair. "Besides, I needed the distraction. Paul and I closed the office all week for Thanksgiving, and Mal's been out of town." He shot me a quicksilver grin. "But he's coming home today."

I laughed and gave him a good-natured shove toward the door. "We'd better get going, then, eh? Don't forget your jacket. Chilly out there."

"Good call." He stretched his back and let out a little groan before grabbing his fleece from the worktable. "I still can't believe you let your sister talk you into renovating this old place, let alone converting it into an event barn." He turned, hands on hips, and surveyed the open space—the rough-hewn ceiling beams that had stood for a hundred years, the metal roof Alana swore was "atmospheric," the walls that had been carefully treated to make the space weather-tight while maintaining as much rustic charm as possible. "You've done an amazing job."

I shrugged, uncomfortable with the praise. "It's come a long way."

"I remember when your granddad kept his vintage planter collection in here. This old barn felt like a museum when I was a kid."

"More like a cemetery of obscure creepy shit," I corrected. I did my customary tour of the barn, unplugging cords and making sure everything was locked up tight. There wasn't much crime in the Thicket, but I'd been stolen from once before, and I wouldn't take chances now. "The ones shaped like human heads still haunt my nightmares."

"Oh, God, those terrified me." Brooks's eyes widened. "Those aren't still around, are they?"

I chuckled. "Nah. My dad got rid of 'em ages ago." I scratched at my beard, which was probably caked with sawdust, and thought longingly of a nice hot shower, an ice-cold beer, and a few hours sacked out on my couch. "Back when he culled Grandad's collection down to a manageable level."

"Would we call it manageable when it still takes up your parents' entire machine shed?" Brooks mused as I hit the lights and we headed for the door.

I snorted. Brooks wasn't wrong. Fortunately, I'd built my own barn five years back to house all the tools and equipment I needed for my nursery business. It was located a quarter mile east of my parents' farmhouse, next to the four long greenhouses that kept me busy during the winter.

I waved a hand dismissively. "Doesn't matter since my dad hasn't been out to the machine shed since the last time he attempted to change his oil, which was right before he remembered how much he hates changing oil. He ended up taking the car to Elmer Nutter's shop over in Dooberville since Elmer's a 'man who knows his way around some hot fluids.'"

Brooks laughed.

I grinned in response as we turned toward the exit. "Since then, Dad either spends his days either up at Bull Lake fishing with your father or across the road at the Ivey place if Ava's bringing the grandkids over for a visit. My parents are dying for a grandchild to spoil, and me and Alana haven't done our duty." I pulled the door closed and jabbed my key in the lock a bit more forcefully than necessary.

Brooks winced. "I feel this pain. My folks haven't let up since Mal and I got married. Big Red and Cindy Ann are getting impatient for more babies, even though Gracie already gave them three."

"At least you're married," I countered, nodding at the band on his left hand and shoving my own hands in my pockets. "My mom and your mom keep making noises about setting me up with a 'nice local boy.' Do you know what it's like when Cindy Ann Johnson and Lurleen Jackson combine forces? Your mom has a mental contacts list of all the queer men in the greater Licking Thicket area, and my mom has an insatiable need to meddle in folks' lives..."

"Oh, God. Together, they're an unstoppable matchmaking force, aren't they?" Brooks shuddered. "Have you considered picking someone on your own?"

I rolled my eyes. *How quickly married people forgot.* "'Picking' a guy? You make it sound like they're pie pumpkins in the patch over at the Albermarles' farm and I can pay by the pound. Or like they're on a shelf at the Feed and Seed, halfway between the t-posts and the riding mowers, and all I have to do is find one I like and plunk down my money. It doesn't work like that."

"Alright," he conceded, chuckling. "I see your point."

I blew out a breath. I was feeling riled and unsettled by the turn in the conversation, and I wasn't sure why. Yes, there were times when I wished I had someone to share my life with, but it wasn't as if I were pining for romance. I was content with my life the way it was.

Mostly.

"It's been a while since I've found someone I was really into, that's all," I explained. I still sounded more defensive than I wanted to. "And before you ask, no, I haven't bothered looking recently, firstly because I've already dated most of the men on your mom's list and secondly because I've got enough on my plate as it is." I gestured toward the mostly renovated barn and then across a field and through the tree break toward my own land and greenhouses. "Getting this event business off the ground while keeping my nursery business thriving is my main focus right now, which means I'm way more interested in finding a guy who knows his way around an orbital sander than a guy who enjoys long walks in the moonlight, if you catch my drift."

Brooks nodded easily, but we both knew I was protesting a little too much, even if he was too kind to point it out.

I cleared my throat. "Anyway. Speaking of men who do manual labor..." I opened my truck door, grabbed my phone from the front seat, and turned back to Brooks. "Do you take Venmo?" I asked.

His forehead creased. "Venmo? For what?"

"You've spent the last four days hauling junk and repairing flooring. That's hard work, and I'm paying you for it. Don't worry," I added quickly. "It's coming out of the event barn budget. Alana's got it all set up."

Brooks shook his head. "Forget it. Tell Alana it's a gift."

"She told me you were gonna say that." I folded my arms over my chest. "And I told *her* I wouldn't take no for an answer, even if I had to sneak the money into your house, one twenty-dollar bill at a time. Might make things a little awkward when I show up in the middle of your reunion with Mal tonight, but I'm sure he'll roll with it. He knows how stubborn you can be."

Brooks sighed and slapped his cap against his leg. A plume of dust puffed into the chilly air. Dark was coming in fast, and I couldn't wait to get home and shower off the grime of the day... along with the residue of this strange mood that had suddenly come over me.

"Actually." Brooks gave me a considering look. "You know what? If you insist on paying me, why not donate to my mom's charity thing? Alana volunteers at the animal shelter, so she'll be good with it."

I shrugged. "How you spend the money is your business. I'll send it to you, and you can—"

"Donate it yourself," Brooks interrupted. "You'll be there tonight, right? You can't miss the Biddin'."

I closed my eyes and groaned. "That's tonight?"

This wasn't really a question. One part of my brain was very aware that the Biddin' always happened on the Tuesday before Thanksgiving, and another part of my brain was very aware that *today* was the Tuesday before Thanksgiving. Somehow, those two parts of my brain had chosen not to communicate, though—possibly out of a sense of self-preservation.

"I'm surprised no one roped you into auctioning yourself off." He winked.

"Alana tried," I admitted. "Gave me a whole song and dance about how the community only thrives if everyone takes part, and blah blah. But I told her I was too busy. I *am* too busy."

"Uh-huh. Well, now you've got extra money, so you can take part as a bidd*er* instead of a bidd*ee*. She can't complain about that." Brooks looked a little too cheerful at this prospect. "Maybe finding a man *is* as easy as buying one."

"Oh, fuck no." I scowled, horrified. "I'm not bidding on a bachelor. Are you kidding?"

"You don't have to bid," Brooks said. "You could just make a straight-out donation. But..." He full-on grinned, making no effort to hide his glee. "We both know your mom will skin you alive if you donate money without creating a little excitement for the good folk of Licking Thicket."

Fuck. I had no response to this since we both knew he was entirely correct.

I kicked a rock in the driveway and watched it skitter across the dirt into the scrubby grass. "I hate this town."

"You *love* this town," he retorted, smacking my arm. "You and my brother are the only people I know who've never once contemplated leaving."

I sighed. He was right—I truly did love it here.

For one thing, I felt incredibly grateful for the bounty my ancestors had provided me and my family on this land. Our large property had sustained the Jackson clan as far back as anyone around here could remember. We owned acres of farmland, old growth and pine forest, three large ponds, and over a mile of river frontage. When I'd gotten the idea to start a flower and houseplant business, my granddad had parceled off several acres for me and helped me earn enough money to fund the first season of seeds and supplies.

And for another... well, I loved the people in this place. Thicketeers were generally a kind and openhearted bunch who meant well, even if their plans sometimes went spectacularly awry. I could even admit to myself that I kinda liked our weird traditions and festivals. Usually.

"Remember, you don't have to bid on someone because you're madly in love with them. I heard Ferdy Gaskins is gonna be in the auction, and you could have him take pictures of the barn as your date," Brooks offered helpfully. "Or you could bid on Melanie Higgins. She's a kickass plumber, and she'd probably help you install new faucets. *Orrrr* you could offer for Vivek Kaur," Brooks added in a sly voice. "I have no idea what he's good at, but word on the street is that he's single, so maybe you could use your date to, you know, *find out.*"

I glared at him. "The apple clearly hasn't fallen far from Cindy Ann's tree, Brooks Johnson."

Brooks laughed unrepentantly as he took his keys from his pocket and jingled them. "I'm just passing on information, Hunter. How you use it is up to you."

"So generous. You know what? I *will* go tonight, but I will not be bidding on a date. Instead, I'll make sure the whole town knows I'm buying two grand worth of castrations in your name. Maybe they'll rename the affair the Brooks Johnson Castration Celebration in your honor."

"You're a true friend." Brooks shot me the bird as he headed for his truck. "Asshole."

"Love you too, boo! Don't say I never gave you nothing."

"Better get washed up and purty," he called back. "I hear Melvin Murkle's up for auction too. He got his dentures polished as soon as my mom asked him to be one of the bachelors. It's fate, really."

I tried unsuccessfully to hold back a laugh. "Tell your mom if Melvin's willing to remove them altogether, I'll pay extra," I called before both of us finally shut our respective vehicle doors.

Then, I headed home for the world's fastest shower and headed over to the community barn.

Apparently, I had a Biddin' to get to.

———

"Why are you wearing a sweater?" my sister greeted me with a suspicious glint in her eyes. "And you smell nice. What's going on?"

"I'm wearing a sweater because it's cold as tits outside, and I smell like Safeguard bar soap because it was better than stinking like sweat and sawdust from the renovation work."

She let out a little squeal of excitement. "Oh! Is the event space almost ready? Can I come see it? Will you meet me out there tomorrow?"

Before I had a chance to answer, our mother came shuffling over in kitten heels and a blinking pumpkin light necklace. Her black curls were sprayed into their usual helmet shape, and her electric-blue eyeliner displayed the heavy-handed effect she adopted for "special occasions."

Fortunately for those who held stock in Maybelline, my mom thought most occasions were "special."

"You have to bid tonight, kids. I insist." Her eyes darted furtively around the room. "Cindy Ann has it from Tucker, who heard it from Carter Rogers, that some bigwig from out of town is planning on outbidding everyone for Quinn Taffet so Quinn can plan his daughter's wedding. Lord knows why Champ didn't object to his man volunteering for the auction, but it's going to help out the charity big-time."

She turned her gaze on me and narrowed her eyes until they looked like electric-blue slashes beneath her dark eyebrows. "According to the pamphlet, there are at least three gay men for sale tonight. This is your opportunity, Hunter. You ain't gettin' any younger, baby doll."

I set my jaw. "You've pointed out every gay man in town to me at least three times," I reminded her. "If I wasn't interested in dating them before, I'm sure as heck not paying for a date with them in front of the whole town."

"Hmph." She sniffed delicately and put her chin in the air. "In that case, perhaps some generous soul will buy one for you. Like a present. Wouldn't that be lovely?"

"No," I said firmly. "It would not. Don't even think about it."

"I didn't say *me*, Hunter, I said *someone*. Possibly someone anonymous who has a vested interest in your happiness." She patted her shellacked curls, as though any of them would ever dare droop out of place.

I opened my mouth to retort, but Alana, ever the peacemaker, cut in. "Just think," she said softly. "If you make your own bid, you could choose some big, strapping SOB, and your 'date' could be refinishing the barn floor. Romantic, eh?"

I snorted. This was very reminiscent of the conversation I'd had with Brooks. I hadn't taken the suggestion seriously when he'd made it, but if it had the added benefit of getting my mother off my back...

"That's not a bad idea," I admitted.

Mom threw up her hands. Orange glitter nail polish caught the light and nearly blinded me. "I give up. The two of you are more interested in proving yourselves clever in the career department than settling down and making a family. I hope you realize that your plants and your event barn and your... your... whatever your next get-rich-quick scheme is will never take care of you in your old age!"

Alana slid her arm through mine and squeezed. "Yes, but wealthy entrepreneurs can afford to hire full-time staff, Mother. And I, for one, would rather have a licensed medical professional looking after me in my sunset years than some resentful br—"

"Kid!" I said, cutting her off before she could provoke our mother into a super-snit. One of Alana's greatest joys was giving our mom the false impression she didn't want children. The truth of the matter was my sister and I both dreamed about marrying and raising families. But we'd wanted to be financially secure first.

Now, though, my nursery business had finally leveled up to the point where I had five full-time employees (and triple that number in the high season), and there was a light at the end of the tunnel with the barn renovation. So maybe it was time to admit—to myself and never, *ever* to my mother—that I did want something more... and that the impossibility of the situation was making me tetchy.

The trouble was, as I'd explained to Brooks, pickings were slim in the Thicket, no matter how many people Cindy Ann had on her roster. I'd grown up with many of the gay men in town, and they felt more like brothers than potential romantic partners. Others had dated my friends over the years, and I knew way too many of their red flags to ever date them myself. Not to mention, the second I set my sights on anyone in the Thicket, I'd practically be inviting the Thicket's busybodies and matchmakers—including my mom—even *further* into my personal business than they'd already invited themselves.

No, thank you.

I'd come up with a different plan. Eventually. But in the meantime...

"I'll bid on someone tonight, Mom," I promised.

She still looked suspicious of my motives—and rightly so—but let out a breath and patted her hair again. "Thank you, Hunter." She turned her narrowed gaze on Alana. "At least *someone* around here cares about their mother."

Thankfully, she stormed off before catching sight of Alana's epic eye roll.

My sister craned her neck to see who was lining up to take the stage for the bachelor and bachelorette presentations.

I'd never bid on anyone before, but I sure as hell had enjoyed watching others do it. The whole town remembered the time Hetty Donaldson paid one dollar for a night with Victor Andréas just to lecture him for three hours on the proper way to slice her roast beef at the deli counter. Or the time Dunn Johnson had bid a thousand dollars to take his own husband on a date and told everyone it was because their pet pig Bernadette was "a sensitive soul who might be confused if she heard Tuck was spending time with another man, and I care too much about my livestock to upset them that way." Or the time Princess Williams paid five hundred bucks so her boyfriend would put up the Christmas lights. Or the year the Powell triplets bid on dates with the Driscoll twins and the mayor insisted the high school math teacher stop the bidding long enough to give a simple math lesson.

No matter what happened—and there was an unspoken

agreement it was all in good fun—it was bound to be entertaining. I knew all these folks, and they knew me, I reminded myself. I needed to stop taking this thing so seriously.

Alana and I made our way up front while having a brief, hushed discussion about which of the "bachelors" on auction we should choose.

"I say go for Gracie Mawbry," Alana insisted as she dragged me through the last of the crowd. "She redid her own floors last year, so she gets the vibe I want, and... *Ooof.* What the heck, Hunter? You stopped so fast I nearly face-planted into the folding chairs. Are you...? *Ohhh.*"

I heard her words like they were coming from a far distance... possibly from a whole other lifetime. Because as the crowd parted in front of her, I spotted a man standing off to the side of the stage dressed in pressed wool trousers that clung to his narrow hips and a white button-down so starched I could use it to stake tomatoes. He was nodding at something Savannah Nutter was saying, and the serious look in his dark eyes was so familiar I recognized him immediately.

"Oh my *God*," Alana breathed. "Is that...?"

"Junior Nutter," I gritted out. My stomach burned, and my chest tightened with a whole mess of emotions too tangled for me to piece them out entirely. Confusion, shock, annoyance, anticipation... and something else. Something that made my mouth water against my will.

"But he *never* comes back here," Alana said, still staring like she'd never seen a beautiful man before. I might have made a snarky comment about this if I weren't busy staring at him the same way.

I forced myself to look away. "Well, clearly he does," I snapped. Though she was right, I couldn't remember the last time I'd heard about Junior visiting the Thicket. It was well-known that he was far too busy with whatever the heck he did in Chicago to care much about the people he'd left behind.

"Bet he could sand the hell out of a floor," Alana whispered.

I elbowed her.

She elbowed me back. "What? Look at those broad shoulders. Don't tell me you wouldn't want him to... sand something of yours too."

"I'm not bidding on Junior Nutter," I hissed. "First off, I don't believe he'd ever participate in something so countri-fied. Mr. Private Boarding School is *way* too hoity-toity to ever let his people sign him up to be auctioned off like a prize steer. *And even if he did,*" I went on when it looked like she was about to argue, "have you forgotten that he's persona non grata in the Jackson family?"

"I haven't forgotten anything," Alana informed me. She straightened her shoulders and flicked back her blonde ponytail with one lacquered nail. "And if you won't bid on him, I will."

I stared at my beautiful sister in horror. "You can't. Alana. Of all the men ever born in the Thicket, Junior is the snottiest, the most entitled, the—"

"Sexiest, the most gorgeous—"

"The sneakiest, the... the... thievingest—"

"The smartest, and... oooh, baby." Still staring at Junior, she bit her lip and wiggled her eyebrows. "Definitely the *ass*-iest. That man has been *blessed.*"

"Ass-iest is not a word," I protested, but I couldn't help turning to see what she was looking at.

Junior had turned and bent a little so his uncle Amos, who wasn't carrying his cane, could sling an arm over his shoulder. The way he was leaning did a lot of interesting, eye-popping things to Junior's posterior region.

"Ass-iest is as much a word as thievingest and *muuuuch* more applicable to the situation," Alana purred. "I know you think Junior stole from you, but I still think there was more to that situation than met the eye. You never found out why—"

I looked away again. "Because I know why. Junior thinks he's better than all of us. He thought he had a right—"

Alana shook her head and patted my arm in a gesture that was more riling than soothing. "Hunter. I love you. But sometimes you tell yourself a story and twist the facts to fit it."

I scowled. "I do *not*—"

Alana didn't want to hear my objections. She'd already turned toward the stage, where Amos Nutter was passing the mic to Red Johnson so the mayor could open the festivities with a moving speech about... castration, I was pretty sure? I couldn't make myself pay attention.

Alana was wrong—dead wrong—about me *and* about Charlton Nutter, Jr.

She seemed to forget that I'd known Junior for years, that we'd gone through elementary and middle school together, that we'd shared a tent on Cub Scout campouts, that Junior had taught me to swim and I'd taught him to ice-skate, that I'd considered the asshole my friend—to the point where I'd thrown down when the kids at school teased Junior about his prim-and-proper polos.

Alana might have forgotten the details of how everything changed too, but I certainly hadn't. At the start of freshman year, Junior's father had married a rich second wife who ponied up some cash. Almost instantly, it seemed like the sweet and slightly geeky kid I'd known had grown a foot taller and started talking crazy talk about the world outside the Thicket, where a person could "be whoever they wanted," like you couldn't simply be who you were right here. Rumors had swirled about Junior's mom buying a house in Nashville so they could move away, and at first, I'd dismissed them—Nutters belonged in the Thicket, just like Jacksons did, so they wouldn't *leave*, for heaven's sake.

But then, the Turkey Incident had occurred.

Afterward, Junior had never apologized. Never explained. Livid and betrayed as I'd been, I'd still expected him to *try*... and I might even have forgiven him. But days had gone by... weeks... a whole month, with us passing silently in the hallway at school or standing awkwardly on a sidewalk while our mothers chatted outside town events, and every time Junior refused to meet my eyes or open his mouth, I got angrier and angrier.

Then one day in late December, my mom finally got tired of my attitude and sat me down for her unique version of a maternal come-to-Jesus. "Hunter, baby," she'd sighed. "My patience is worn through, so you gotta let this go. Who knows why Junior did what he did? Maybe he took a wild hair and tried to play a joke. Or maybe he's taking after his daddy and got above his raisin' once he knew he was going off to his chichi private boarding school next semester." She'd rolled her eyes. "Don't matter either way 'cause it's over and done now. Junior and his mom left town yesterday. They moved on to greener pastures, and it's time you moved on too. So no more stomping around the house. You're riling the dogs to barking, and it's working my nerves. Hear me?"

I'd heard her... at least, up to the part where she'd said Junior was gone. After that, I'd been too choked with red-hot emotion to take much in. Junior had left me—I mean, left *the Thicket*—without making things right or even muttering a "goodbye and good luck"? The boy I'd considered my friend would never have done that. So... maybe my mom had hit the nail on the head. Maybe Junior thought he was better than the rest of us. Maybe Junior had never cared about me—I mean, *the Thicket*.

Maybe I'd never actually known the real Junior at all.

Over time, it became clear I was right because Junior never returned to the Thicket, at least that I knew of. He'd shaken the dust of the town off his feet for good and leveled up to his fancy private boarding school, his fancy college, his fancy *life*, where I'd bet he never worked up an honest sweat for an honest day's work like the rest of us did or spent a single minute thinking about the people he'd left behind.

Until now.

The more I thought about this, the madder I got, so that by the time the auction had gotten underway and Junior had, to my surprise, taken his place onstage with the other volunteers, I was so consumed with the injustice of it all that I couldn't stop staring at him.

You couldn't just leave that way and then come back all these years later like the Thicket's own prodigal son. Sure, Brooks Johnson had done it, but that was *different*. Brooks had reasons for going and reasons for coming home. Brooks was an upstanding guy who cared about people. Brooks wasn't up on the auction block, smiling his big, fake smile, parading his strong shoulders and luscious ass in front of the whole town, making the old men laugh at his antics and the ladies—including my own damn sister!—swoon and sigh and reach for their debit cards.

Junior Nutter needed to be taught a lesson. A lesson that did not involve him spending his "date" shooting the shit with Skeets Miller about the Bears' chances of making it to the playoffs, or letting Dot Johnson force-feed him pumpkin pie while she crocheted him a lap blanket, or—worst of all—taking my sister to the Steak and Bait for tater tots, which was exactly the scenario my mother would engineer if Alana actually won him. No way was I going to let that happen.

So when Amos Nutter opened the bidding for Junior at a buck, I grabbed the placard from Alana's hand, raised it as high as I could, and bid my entire two thousand dollars all in one go.

The moment I spoke, a stunned hush fell over the entire community barn, and all heads turned to gawp at me. My face went burning hot, which momentarily stopped the angry *whooshing* of my pulse in my ears, my throat went dry and itchy, and all at once, I came back to myself...

And very much wished I hadn't.

"Lurleen, is that your boy?" someone demanded in a hushed voice.

"What's Hunter want with Junior Nutter?" someone else muttered.

"Picked him like a pumpkin in the patch," a voice I strongly suspected was Brooks crowed. "Now, *that's* some town excitement."

"Oooh, wait, wasn't there bad blood—?"

"*Mmm*hmm. Must be fifteen years ago now, but who could forget—?"

"The Incident!" a voice stage-whispered. "*The Great Thicket Turkey Incident.*"

"I always said it was a *foul* prank. Get it? Because turkeys are fowls—"

"I don't understand. What was the Incident?" a sweet, bewildered voice asked.

"Don't worry, Parrish, I'll tell you all about it at the play-ground tomorrow," a voice that sounded like Ava Siegel assured him. "I'm sure *everyone* will be talking about it."

The whispers rose to a crescendo, and the weight of so many eyes on me made me want to jump out of my skin.

Christ on a cracker. What had I done?

Amos Nutter stepped toward the front of the stage and shielded his eyes from the lights so he could see me. "Dang, Hunter! I didn't even have a chance to read the part of Junior's bio that says he's gay. Do you have gold-star gaydar, or do you gay folks just recognize each other or somethin'? Either way... *sold!* Junior's all yours."

Wait. *Wait.* Junior was gay? So then everyone must be thinking I'd bid on him because...?

"Holy cannoli," Alana leaned over to murmur in my ear. "I was just teasing you about bidding on Junior... and I guess you were teasing when you said you wouldn't, huh? You just became a Biddin' legend, Hunter, and snagged yourself a date with a hot, rich, gay Nutter to boot! The ladies of the Thicket will be talking about this for weeks." She grinned and knocked her shoulder into mine. "You gave Mom her Christmas present a little early this year."

Oh, *shit.*

My breath started coming faster and faster, and I turned away. I needed space. I needed fresh air. I needed—

I turned on my heel and bolted straight out of the community barn into the dark, cold night.

I needed to puke.

Chapter Three

Charlton

I STARED at the double doors Hunter Jackson—a very grown-up and apparently *gay* Hunter Jackson—had just slammed through.

What the hell was happening?

Emmaline, who was working the donations table at the front of the room, waved a hand at Hunter's retreating form. "Thanks for your winning bid, sweetie! Don't forget to send your payment to ProudNutter@castrationsociety.org!"

The same lady who'd nudged me into the center of the stage only a minute ago now nudged me toward the steps. "Move along, darlin'. Your cousin Kandi's up next, and she always goes for a pretty penny." She leaned in and lowered her voice. "Sings like a songbird, she does. Men are suckers for a lovely voice."

I glanced at Kandi, one of the five billion Nutter cousins, who was all done up in a skintight cocktail dress that hugged her generous figure, plus full Marilyn Monroe hair and makeup. "Right. Definitely her voice."

Kandi and I had never been close, but as I passed her,

she shot me a knowing wink and tilted her head toward the doors where Hunter had disappeared. "Good luck, sugar. That one's always been a handful, hasn't he?"

I nodded vaguely as I made my way down the stage steps. Hunter Briggs Jackson, pride of the Jackson clan, heir to one of the largest landholdings in Middle Tennessee, beloved child of a fiercely protective mother whose eyeliner would be forever seared into my brain, *had* always been a handful.

We'd started out as friends in the way that all boys in the Thicket of the same age start out as casual friends, but something about Hunter had always drawn me to him. He'd been what Thicketeers would call a "boy's boy": confident and protective, hardheaded and competitive, hot-tempered and kindhearted, the kid everyone wanted on their team. I remembered being absurdly happy that he often seemed to pick *me* as his partner in crime, especially since I'd been on the shorter side back then, and I (or at least my dad) tended to be the butt of a lot of middle school jokes. In fact, if I were being honest, I'd idolized Hunter Jackson, in a classic "Do I want to *be* him or to be *with* him?" kind of way.

I'd solved that riddle pretty comprehensively in the spring of eighth grade after Hunter had bulked up from all the landscaping work he'd been doing around town to earn extra money after his family had a few hard seasons on their farm, and my heart had started beating double time every time I caught a glimpse of him. All that summer, I'd been a heart-eyed mess, pining over my friend's string-bean biceps and peach-fuzz facial hair, hanging on every story he told me, stammering out my own confusion about my dad's remarriage and soaking up the comfort he gave me, desperately wanting him to know how I felt about him while praying he never would.

Eighth grade, man. Fucking *awful.*

But worse than that was what happened that autumn when we'd finally started high school—the mortifying, misguided, misunderstood clusterfuckery that locals had apparently dubbed the Great Thicket Turkey Incident but which I privately thought of as "The Time I Learned That No Good Deed Goes Unpunished." After that, there were no more heart-eyes, no more friendship, only disillusionment and dislike—hatred, really—until my mom and I moved away after Christmas.

That dislike had been mutual too. No doubt about it. So why the hell had Hunter just bid an exorbitant amount of money to win a date with his mortal enemy?

"Congratulations, Junior!" My cousin Ollie stepped into my path with a beaming smile. "The whole family's real proud of you for scoring such a huge donation."

"And don't worry at all about what Hunter's gonna make you do on your date," his wife, Kendra, added with total sincerity. "I mean, sure, he's probably got fifteen years of built-up anger about the Incident, and he's probably gonna take it out through your blood, sweat, and tears by forcing you to do the worst kind of manual labor he can think up, but... I mean... think of how many dogs'll be spayed and neutered thanks to you!"

"Lovely," I muttered as understanding dawned and, with it, no small amount of anger. "That's just... lovely. Will you excuse me?"

Without waiting for their reply, I wound my way through the crowd, ignoring their whispered comments, and pushed open the doors to the front of the community center.

The late-autumn night was cold, especially after the warmth of the crowded space. Golden fairy lights, which had been festooned around the pumpkin-and-hay-bale-strewn entryway, swayed drunkenly in the chilly breeze, haphazardly sending beams of light into the darkness of the parking area like the flashes of a lighthouse. And it was in one of these flashes that I saw my overgrown, coward-ass former friend striding toward his truck on the far side of the lot.

"Stop!" I cried, jogging toward him. "You can't just fuck off without explaining yourself, Hunter. What the hell was that about?"

Hunter paused, squared his shoulders, but didn't turn around. "Shut up, Junior."

"Make me," I retorted like we were still eleven. Embarrassed heat washed over me. "Or better still, tell me why you just bid a shit-ton of money for a date with—"

"Not a *date*." Hunter whirled around. Up close, the dancing lights revealed a handsome, bearded face that was all firm planes and hard angles where it had once been round with youth, along with a heavily muscled frame beneath his fitted sweater that was easily twice as muscular as it had been last time I'd seen him.

Devastating, I thought helplessly.

Then, Hunter went on. "You are the last person I'd want to date."

I forced myself to stop imagining what his pecs looked like beneath the sweater and told myself that since I hadn't been an eighth grader for a decade and a half, Hunter's pronouncement could not possibly sting as much as it felt like it did.

"Well, good! Because I wouldn't want to date you either." I lifted my chin. "In fact, I... I'd want it even *less* than you!"

"Good."

"Great!"

"*Excellent.*"

"So why'd you bid on me, then?" I demanded. "Is this some kind of revenge ploy? Because it's a really expensive one, especially since you're leaving without even making arrangements for whatever shit job you plan to have me do."

I kept telling myself to shut up—I didn't actually *want* him to make arrangements. I had no burning desire to do physical labor *or* to spend time with someone who clearly hated my guts—but something in me wanted to provoke him.

"Or did you do that thing you used to do when we were kids, where you got so flustered, your mouth started saying shit before your brain caught up?" I asked snidely. "Temper, temper, Hunter Jackson."

Hunter made a choking noise, and his pale cheeks flushed dark above his beard. "I said shut up! For fuck's sake, what are you even doing here? I thought Licking Thicket was horse shit on your boot heel. The big, wide world was gonna treat you *so* much better. And you clearly don't give a crap about anyone you left behind. You didn't even come back for Amos's wedding! So why the hell were you up on that auction stage tonight?"

"I think it's pretty standard for people to visit their loved ones at Thanksgiving." I folded my arms over my chest and tried to act casual, as though his accusations—especially the bit about Uncle Amos—hadn't scored a direct hit, the embers of anger in my gut hadn't flared to brilliant flames, and I wasn't strangely (annoyingly) aroused by his proximity after all these years.

"Love," he sneered. "Right."

That made me well and truly angry. "Don't you dare presume to know how I feel about my family," I said in a hard voice. "You don't know shit about me."

Hunter seemed to deflate at this, whether because he regretted his words or for some other reason I couldn't fathom. "That's the damn truth. Tomorrow morning. Eight o'clock. Meet me at the main barn next to my dad's house. We're gonna be refinishing floors." He looked me up and down, inspecting my well-tailored slacks and button-down like I was a cheap cut of beef. His lip curled. "You might want to wear something a little less precious. Something fit to work in... assuming you remember what hard work looks like."

I stared at him, too stunned to reply—was he calling me lazy?—and he *hmphed* as though he'd expected nothing less. Then he turned toward his truck, adding a smug little swagger to his step that made his butt look—

"And stop staring at my ass!" he called over his shoulder as he pulled open his door.

Caught, I gasped. "How did you...? I-I mean... *you wish!*" I yelled, forcing my eyes up. "I have no interest in your ass, Jackson. Like, zero. Less than zero! Negative interest. If I was stranded on a desert island, dying of starvation, and your ass was my only means of survival, I wouldn't... uh..." I trailed off.

"Eat it?" Hunter turned toward me again, and the light from inside the truck showed that his eyes were bright with amusement. "You're saying you'd rather starve than eat my ass? Now, that's a choice. I'm not sure how I ended up on the island with you or why you think I'd be the one getting eaten in this scenario, but it's good to know you wouldn't compromise your standards."

"Fuck off." It was harder than it should have been not to

remember I was angry when I wanted to grin back at him, to share in his amusement, to let myself enjoy the kind of teasing banter we'd shared when we were kids.

But it had always been this way with him, really. Being around him made me feel like I was on a roller coaster—and not one of the ones that had been through any kind of safety inspection in the past fifty years. A rickety old wooden one, the kind that forced you to take your life into your own hands just to experience the wobbly dips and swoops on rusted rails.

Just as I lost the battle and felt my face crack into a smile, the teasing light in Hunter's eyes went out.

"You're a *turkeynapper*," he accused, like he was reminding us both of this fact. "A thief."

"Oh, for fuck's sake. I am not." I rolled my eyes. "It's been fifteen years—"

"I haven't forgotten," he said grimly. "And I haven't forgiven."

"Forgiven? Are you serious? I wasn't stealing your turkey. I was trying to... Ugh. Never mind. Just... get a life, Hunter. Jesus."

"I have a life, *Junior*. It's here in the Thicket, and you're not part of it. We're not friends, and the only thing I want from you is hard labor. Tomorrow morning, don't be late."

With that, he hopped in the truck, slammed the door, and revved the engine before pulling out onto the street.

I stared after him.

"Charlton," I muttered under my breath. "My name is *Charlton*."

I turned back to the community center and wondered whether I had the guts to go back inside and face all the questions. The sheer number of people who wanted to refer to me as Junior made me want to punch something...

and the thing I wanted to punch the most had just driven away.

Instead, I wandered over to my cousin's SUV and let myself in before pulling out my phone and dialing my best friend back in the city.

"Charlie, you haven't even lasted a full twenty-four hours," Seamus said in lieu of a greeting. "No, you can't catch an early flight home, or your mother is going to wind up living in the Waldorf's spa permanently, and it'll bankrupt you."

"It's not that," I said, even though the thought of inventing a work emergency and fleeing the state had definitely crossed my mind. "You're never going to believe what just happened."

I gave him a quick rundown of the small-town shenanigans—pausing for a long, eye-rolling moment while he laughed his head off at the very idea of the Biddin'—and the unexpected, obscenely large single bid from an unexpected player.

"Wait... Hunter Jackson? As in *the* Hunter? The guy you told me about that night back in college when you were drunk and listening to Adele? The one with the turk—"

"Yes," I interrupted before he could remind me of the depths of my patheticness. "Him."

"Ooooh. We loves Hunter."

"No. We hates him."

Seamus made a noise of disagreement in his throat. "Eh. I've always thought that was one of those cases of Shakespearean denial. Protesting too much because you actually want his dick."

"Pfft. I do *not* want his dick."

My tone wasn't convincing, even to me, and the lie sat between us like a dick-shaped fib of epic proportions.

Seamus whistled slowly. "Wow. I was right. In fact, you're mentally lubing that puppy right now. Tell me I'm lying."

I groaned and shifted in my seat. There was no way I was going to (admit to) fantasize(ing) about Hunter Jackson's cock.

I swallowed thickly. "Can we refocus, please? What do I do now? Hunter's definitely not interested in *me*. For God's sake, the man insinuated that I'm lazy and that I think I'm too good for my own family." My pulse of frustrated anger at this was nearly enough to kill off my lust. "He could be the love child of Chris Hemsworth and Timothée Chalamet with a dick like John Holmes, and I still wouldn't be prepared to show up there and... and... *refinish his floors*."

"Huh. You make that sound like a euphemism."

I almost wished it was a euphemism. "It's not."

"Can we be sure, though? Because everything in that wackadoo town is a double entendre, so it's possible—"

"Seamus!"

"Fine, fine. If you're not *refinishing his floors*, then I guess you're... refinishing his floors. Ba-dum-bum."

My exhale made a white cloud in the air between the driver and passenger seat. "I hate you."

"The same way you hate Hunter Jackson and Licking Thicket?" he teased.

"I don't *hate* the Thicket. I just... don't... belong here," I muttered. "I never did."

"Sure. Because it's backward and ridiculous and filled with Jacksons and Nutters," he said reasonably. "You can't live the life you want in a place like that."

"Maybe not *backward*," I argued, as though Seamus wasn't repeating things he'd heard from me over the years.

"Turns out they might be more accepting than I remembered." I hesitated. "But the rest is true enough. There's at least one too many Jacksons in this town."

"Uh-huh." He chuckled. "But really, Charlie, how bad could your 'date' be? It'll get you one step closer to winning that stupid bet with your mom, and if you're busy refinishing Hunter's floors—in whatever way we interpret that—at least you won't have to spend the entirety of Thanksgiving-Eve-Day at the farmhouse with your extended family."

"I wouldn't anyway," I said, remembering the sign I'd seen earlier. "Tomorrow is the Licking Thicket Stuffin'."

"The... what?"

As I explained another of the Thicket's hokey traditions, Seamus laughed so hard I was legitimately concerned he might choke himself.

"It's not that funny," I informed him, as though I hadn't had the same amused-horror reaction when I'd been reminded of the event. "It's just a chance for the town to swap... well, *stuff*. Thanksgiving stuff. Casseroles. Pies. Congealed salads."

"What kind of salad?"

"Congealed? It's made with different kinds of Jell-O, and usually pineapple chunks or cranberries, and sometimes mayonnaise or cottage cheese or marshmallows, and... You know what? Never mind."

"Dear God in heaven." Seamus let out a shuddering breath. "That might be the most troubling thing you've said yet. Licking Thicket is trying to poison you."

"It's not so bad," I admitted, not sure if I was talking about the food or the town. "Better than spending time with Hunter Jackson in any capacity."

When I said the words, I actually meant them. But two hours later, when I'd returned to Amos's house and found that the whole family had congregated there for a spontaneous, raucous celebration of my new reputation as "the most expensive waste of a bid in Biddin' history," I decided maybe Seamus was right.

Maybe spending the day doing manual labor for Hunter Jackson *was* better than having to attend the Stuffin' with these Nutters. Like Seamus had said, how bad could it be?

Chapter Four

Hunter

I DIDN'T COME up with my brilliant scheme until I'd gotten home from the Biddin' and consumed a quantity of Dickel that had made even my silent thoughts sound whiskey-slurred. By that point, I'd convinced myself that Junior Nutter had provoked me into bidding on him the same way he'd provoked me into getting half-hard for him in the parking lot later—drunk logic didn't require me to contemplate *how* he'd done either of those things, which was why it was superior to all other forms of logic—and it was therefore also Junior's fault that the entire Thicket would be taking a renewed interest in my romantic business when I'd actively been trying to avoid the spotlight for years.

Refinishing floors was too easy for him, I decided. Junior deserved payback in kind.

So, I'd sent out a few drunken texts.

Remarkably enough, in the too-bright light of day the following morning, my idea still seemed nearly as brilliant as it had the night before... though, admittedly, I wasn't known for being clearheaded when it came to Junior

Nutter, even without the hangover headache throbbing behind my eyes.

"Here," my sister said, shoving an old duffle bag at my chest. "Don't tell anyone where you got it."

I stood at my kitchen counter in nothing but pajama pants and a first-sip coffee haze. I'd long ago stopped bitching at her about barging in without knocking. I glanced down at the bag. "Why not?"

"Because it's the mascot costume from St. Mary's in Memphis. Don't ask me how I ended up with it—it's a long story, and I'd prefer you retain plausible deniability if anyone recognizes the famous Lady Turkey."

"*Lady* Turkey?"

"Yeah. It's a girls' school. Don't worry, though, the costume's man-sized. There's a pair of tights that are really stretchy, and then he can just step into the actual costume part and zip it up. There's a headpiece in there and shoe coverings too. My senior year at Rhodes, one of the defensemen wore it for a joke, and if a defenseman can fit into it, Junior sure can."

I didn't bother commenting that a football player at her tiny private college didn't necessarily imply large or muscular or that the Junior I'd met last night had been distractingly *both*.

"Thanks." I set the bag on the counter. "For the costume and for, you know, getting on board with my plan."

"Your plan, in which you're not actually going out on a romantic-type date with the handsome Nutter you bid on but instead forcing him to dress up like a turkey in front of the whole town as vengeance, which may or may not make Mom so disappointed she'll poison our Thanksgiving dinner?" Alana grinned, unconcerned, and inspected her manicure. "Anything for you, Hunter. But I'm planning to avoid the giblet gravy tomorrow, just in case."

Shit. When she put it that way...

I hesitated. "I should probably be having second thoughts about this, right?"

She glanced up in surprise. "Second thoughts? Heck no. I think you're doing the right thing. This'll be the apology you've wanted for fifteen years. You'll get it over with once and for all, then the two of you can move on. End your little feud."

I squinted at her in confusion. "What makes you think we'll be moving on?"

"Hunter, come on. He took your turkey a million years ago—"

"My *prize* turkey," I corrected.

Alana pinched the bridge of her nose. "Dolly never won a prize since he wasn't present for the competition, remember? That was the whole point. Junior took the bird, then brought him back after the competition was already finished. Anyway, once you parade Junior around dressed up in this, you'll have to admit the score will be even."

I didn't have to admit it. I didn't have to admit anything. I didn't have to forgive him at all. *Ever.* And I wouldn't.

I took a deliberate sip of coffee so none of that would come out of my mouth. "You gonna be in town to see the show?"

"Obviously. You know how the Jackson family feels about the Stuffin', Hunter." She rolled her eyes. "There are so many of us attending this year that we have to take it in shifts so we don't overwhelm everyone. I told Caroline Pickett I'd stand at her table and help her hand out her cranberry sauce."

I thought of the gourmet-flavored sauces Caroline liked

to make every year and winced. "Has she not realized no one wants that stuff? It's tasty, but real cranberry sauce is can-shaped and jiggles. Everyone knows this."

She shrugged. "Try telling that to someone who went to the Culinary Institute."

"She went to the *Louisiana* Culinary Institute," I said. "She seems to always leave that detail out."

"Doesn't matter. Anyway, I'll see you there. Don't get murdered before I have a chance to see that man dressed up like a turkey."

"Pfft. I'm not scared of Junior Nutter," I assured her.

But when I made my way over to the barn and informed Junior that my plan for him had changed, the anger in his dark eyes almost made me want to run and hide.

Almost.

"You want me to *what?*"

"You heard me," I said. My heart was beating a mile a minute, but I'd be damned if I let him see that. "You're going to put on this turkey outfit and sit your ass down at the Stuffin' while holding a sign confessing to your crimes."

"My crimes?"

I began ticking them off on each finger. "Unlawful Seizure of a Domestic Fowl. Nefarious Interference in the Fair and Proper Execution of a 4-H Competition. Criminal Trespass. Disorderly Conduct. Public Indecency."

The edge of one of his lips turned up. "Public indecency?"

"You think stealing someone's prize bird isn't indecent? Well, it was. *Is.*"

"Public indecency generally involves nudity."

I shot him a look. "For all I know, you were naked during the commission of the crime, Junior!"

He gritted his teeth. "My name isn't Junior. It's Charlton. Occasionally Charlie. Okay?"

That caught me off guard. "Is this one of your big-city airs? You've always been called Junior—"

"No. I haven't. My family called me Junior because my father is also Charlton Nutter, and the whole town followed along, but I was *never* okay with it. I tried to correct every teacher and coach for years. It wasn't until I left the Thicket that I actually got to be called by my own name."

I opened my mouth to mock him, but his fierce expression stopped me. "Fine, then. Charlton."

He rolled his eyes. "And I didn't commit any crimes—"

"You stole Dolly Parton!" I yelled just a little too loud.

He blinked at me. "Pardon?"

"My turkey, Dolly Parton," I said with a huff. "Did you, or did you not, bird-nap him out of his turkey habitat right before the 4-H Thanksgiving Turkey Showmanship Competition, when you *knew* I'd spent five months raising him from a tiny poult?"

He looked away guiltily. "Would you believe I, um... borrowed him?"

"No." I pointed at the duffle bag on the floor between us angrily. "Turkey costume. Now."

"I brought Dolly back!" he insisted.

"Four hours in the town square while you gobble for forgiveness. That's our date, Nutter. Make it happen." I strode off across the wide expanse of unfinished barn floor to the storeroom, where I'd stashed the sign I'd made.

When I came back out, Juni... *Charlton* Nutter had been replaced by a six-foot-tall, brown-feathered turkey with a homicidal look in his eyes. When he lifted his arms in a gesture of extreme annoyance, the attached orange and red tail feathers spread out in an arc on both sides. "You happy now?"

I bit back a giddy giggle-snort. "Not quite, but I'm getting there."

He let out a long-suffering sigh. "Let's get this over with."

I shoved the sign at him. "Here. Get in the truck."

———

"What are you up to, Hunter?" Dunn Johnson demanded, stepping right into my prime turkey viewing location: a spot right under the big lamp post at the main entrance to the town square, where the Stuffin' was already underway.

"Nothing that concerns you. Mind your business." I waved him to one side. "You're blocking my view."

Dunn jabbed a finger at Charlie—I'd decided halfway to town that I couldn't call a man under the age of a hundred "Charlton" with a straight face—and the gaggle of townsfolk who'd paused in their mission to collect assorted Thanksgiving side dishes so they could appreciate the giant turkey in their midst. Then he turned back to me and glared some more. "You're responsible for that spectacle, and you think it ain't my business?"

"I'm just making sure everyone, including Charlie, knows what he did. He's a criminal. Case closed."

For a moment, we both watched as Charlie walked an invisible picket line up and down the sidewalk on this side of the square, muttering halfhearted *gobble-gobbles*. Every once in a while, a passing driver would honk, and Charlie would raise his sign, making the brightly colored feathers on his arms and tail flutter.

All in all, I felt I had a lot to be thankful for this Thanksgiving.

"His sign says, 'Junior Nutter stole Hunter Jackson's turkey,'" Dunn pointed out, leaning against the lamp post beside me.

"So it does. I painted it myself. What's your point?"

"The point is, if you're tryna embarrass the man, you're failing. How's it possible for someone to look that dang sexy in a turkey costume?"

I shoved Dunn's arm. "It's *not*. Not possible at all. In fact..."

I darted another glance at Charlie. Alana had been correct that the costume fit him... sort of. The headpiece, which tied with a bright blue bow where his wattle should be, fit fine, and the turkey feet that covered his boots were okay, but the main body of the costume—a large, be-feathered leotard with a front zipper—hugged his body like a second skin, and the way his tights clung to his hard thighs was vaguely pornographic.

Or maybe not so vaguely.

I swallowed hard. "He's not sexy. He's hideous."

"Mmm. Hideous," Dunn agreed. "The legs especially. You know, I've always been partial to drumsticks."

I shoved him again, harder this time. "You're a married man," I reminded him.

"No shit. And *that* is my beloved husband." He grinned and tilted his chin toward Tucker, who was standing with the crowd a short distance away, all glassy-eyed and slack-jawed as he watched Charlie march. "Tuck's probably daydreaming about Amazon Priming us a turkey getup of our own," he added fondly.

"Charlton Nutter Junior is a criminal," I said, just to

remind us both that the sexy turkey was actually a horrible human being.

"Oh, right. Because he stole your bird—a *tom* turkey inexplicably named Dolly Parton—a million years ago." Dunn nodded solemnly. "He ruined your life."

I opened my mouth to agree before I realized Dunn was being sarcastic. "You wouldn't understand," I said with a sniff.

"Oh, I understand plenty. Did it ever occur to you to ask him why he did it?"

"I didn't need to. The man got above his raisin', that's all. He decided the Thicket wasn't good enough for him, and he was leaving, so he didn't care who he hurt." I crossed my arms over my chest. "It might sound like a joke to you, but Dolly was important to me, and Charlie knew it, but he took him anyway."

"'Above his raisin'," Dunn repeated. He gave a low whistle. "Don't you sound like the town gossips when they're on a tear."

"What's that supposed to mean?" I demanded.

"Nothin'. Just that I wonder how that idea got in your head, that's all. And why you decided it was true."

"I didn't *decide*—"

"Do you remember why you cared so much about that 4-H competition?" Dunn interrupted. It was clear he thought he already knew the answer.

Charlie must have realized we were talking about him because I caught him marching slowly as he passed us, trying to get closer. I shuffled around until he faced my back, and then I lowered my voice. "Because I wanted to win. I knew I'd raised the best damn bird around."

"Sure," Dunn said calmly. "But winning mattered to you because you wanted to become a turkey farmer. You had strong feelings about free-range heritage breeds at the time, and you wanted to pad your resume. Remember?"

"Turkey *rancher*, Dunn. Jesus," I corrected without thinking. It was shameful for a Thicket boy not to know the difference between a farm and a ranch. The man was a dairy farmer, for God's sake... *Wait.*

"But the following year, you had a crisis of conscience and changed your mind," Dunn went on. "That's when you changed your 4-H focus to agriculture and entered your zinnias."

I could feel Charlie creeping closer again, so I barked over my shoulder, "Gobble louder, turkey! Gobble like you mean it!"

When I turned back to Dunn, I could see he was trying not to laugh. "Shut up," I mumbled.

"Those zinnias won every prize at the fair that year," he continued. "You got written up in the paper, and somebody posted it on a flower blog, and that lady from Maine found out and tried to order the whole kit and caboodle of 'em for her Box Day event, whatever the hell that is." He snorted. "I swear, Northerners have the weirdest names for shit."

"How do you remember all this?" I demanded. Of all the people in the town to have an encyclopedic memory for details, I would not have picked easygoing, fun-loving Dunn.

"'Cause I remember thinking at the time how that Nutter did you a favor." He nodded at Charlie over my head. "If he hadn't done what he did, would you have ended up where you are, running the nicest plant farm in Middle Tennessee?"

"Well. I don't know." I blinked. "But..."

"You don't give a shit about that turkey anymore, Hunter. Not really. So what are you doing making this poor man spend one of his vacation days strutting around in a turkey catsuit when he should be enjoying his time in the Thicket?"

I peeked over my shoulder at the large, arm-flapping nuisance behind me. He'd paused his marching and was now gobbling to the tune of "Stayin' Alive," complete with hip-thrusting disco moves. A bunch of kids and their parents cheered him on, enjoying the free entertainment.

I gritted my teeth. "He left the Thicket," I told Dunn. "He deserves to suffer."

Dunn squeezed my arm almost sympathetically. "He deserves to be welcomed back to the Thicket in a way that doesn't make him terrified to return," he said gently. "Do you have any idea how long Amos planned and schemed to get Junior here? He reached a low point when he spelled out his prayers in cows. Remember the WE LOVE YOU JUNIOR, COME BACK debacle?"

I nodded, remembering the fateful day when I headed to the tractor supply store and saw how the herd in Amos Nutter's pasture had rearranged themselves. "I still say Joanie Brightly was overreacting. A grown woman, running into a muddy field and flapping her arms, trying to make the cows scatter?"

"You might, too, if the cows were spelling JOANIE COCK LOVER," Dunn said reasonably.

Dunn had a point, and not just about Joanie Brightly. Charlie had already despised the Thicket so much he'd barely been home in fifteen years. After today, there was no way he'd show his turkey-thieving face in the Thicket again.

And for some reason, that thought made my stomach twist with discomfort.

For Amos's sake, naturally.

"Okay," I grumbled. "You win." I turned and yanked on

one of Charlie's tail feathers until he stopped. "Show's over, turkey. You're done."

"Hey! Let the bird dance!" Monster, the aptly nick-named vice president of the Devoted Dogs MC, called, shooting me a glower. He draped an arm over Jenn Shipley's shoulders. "My old lady's loving it."

"The rest of us are too," Wade Petersen piped up. He blushed deeply and gestured toward his toddler daughter. "I-I mean... the kids are."

I narrowed my eyes. I knew Wade because he was friends with Diesel and Parrish Partridge, and I'd been under the impression he was straight, but I was starting to wonder, given the way he was ogling my turkey—which was to say, the man wearing the turkey costume *I'd provided*, I mentally corrected. *Not* that I was feeling possessive over Charlie Nutter and his drumsticks in any way.

Christ.

"I was just about to show them my turkey twerk," Charlie said with a grin. In a lower voice, he added, "I haven't been ogled this much since I wore a mesh tank and booty shorts to Chicago Pride. And here I thought the Thicket was a Grindr dead zone." He winked at me, and the uncomfortable twist in my stomach turned into a fiery caval-cade of restless stallions.

"Nobody wants..." I waved my hand in an air circle, indicating his entire turkey-fied being. "Any of this. Believe me."

Charlie looked me up and down. "Hm. *Should* I believe you? Not sure."

Dunn shoved me to one side. "Definitely don't believe him. When he was watching you shake your tail feathers, Hunter was practically vibrating with repressed—*mmpfh!*"

I smacked a hand over Dunn's mouth. "Rage," I told

Charlie. "Repressed rage." I shoved Dunn as far from Charlie as possible. "Nice to see you, Dunn," I said in a fake cheerful voice. "Always a pleasure. Now, go find someone else to harass. Happy holidays."

He mumbled a protest against my fingers, but I didn't pull my hand away until I was sure he'd stopped talking.

When I turned back, I dusted off my hands and noticed Charlie had already dropped his sign. "Let's go. If we leave now, there should still be plenty of time left in my 'date' to sand the barn floors."

He crossed his arms in front of his chest, which made the rows of attached feathers fan in an arc across the front of his body. "You're not actually going to make me sand floors after all this, are you?"

I blinked at him with the innocence of a lamb. "Obviously. You're still on my time, and I paid for you fair and square."

"You make it sound dirty."

I thought of the acres of wood floors that still needed hand-sanding all along the edges. "Oh, it'll be dirty, alright. No doubt about that."

Charlie sighed. "Fine. Let me go tell Amos and my mom I'm heading out first. I promised I'd say hi to them."

I let him lead the way into the square, where the Beautification Corps, who must've been working overtime, had transformed the open lawn into a festive community gathering practically overnight. Long folding tables covered in bright, autumn-printed cloths had been arranged in rows, almost like the booths at the Lickin' artists' fair or the stalls at the weekly farmer's market. In this case, though, every table or group of tables was assigned to a family, and each family had prepared stacks upon stacks of their favorite secret-recipe Thanksgiving side dishes to be handed out for free to anyone else in the community.

Dining room tables around the Thicket were going to be groaning tomorrow under the weight of it all, and not a single person in town would be complaining, either, because the smell of the place was—

"Oh *fuck*, that's good." Charlie ran a hand over his stomach and groaned in a needy way that put thoughts in my head. "I want it all inside me right now."

I tightened my hands into fists as mental images seared themselves into my brain. "Trot along, Butterball. We're on the clock here."

But of course, it wasn't that easy. Charlie got stopped by every Thicketeer we passed so they could smile and compliment him on his costume. At the looooong-ass row of Jackson family tables—where none of my immediate family members were currently stationed, thank fuck—a couple of my great-uncles actually got teary-eyed while patting Charlie on the shoulder and praising how "authentically" he represented the "heart of the Stuffin'."

My family took this festival way, way too seriously.

When we got to the Nutters' table—impressively long, but not nearly long as the Jacksons'—they all teased Charlie good-naturedly until he gave a reprisal of his disco turkey dance routine. Emmaline told Charlie his "plumage is magnificent, sweetie, and puts me in mind of your uncle Amos when he was your age," which made Amos beam so bright his mustache quivered, like Christmas had come early. It was harder than it should have been to rush Charlie along when I could feel him blossoming under the attention.

Charlie's mom, who wore a luxurious cashmere sweater set my mother would have traded one of her children for (probably *me* once she heard what I'd been up to today), stood a little ways behind the table, like she was included but not really part of the action. She watched Charlie with a warm smile and a glint in her eye that would've immediately sent up red flags for *scheming* if she'd still lived in the Thicket but for all I knew was just the way all moms in Nashville looked at their giant turkey sons. Besides, I couldn't imagine what Ms. Nutter had to scheme about.

From time to time, as we stood there, she turned her warm smile on me too, and that made me squirm just a little. Charlie's mom had always been kind to me back in the day, and I wondered what she thought about the way I'd chosen to spend our date.

When we finally escaped the Nutters and I tried to turn us toward the parking lot, I spotted Alana standing at Caroline's table on the other side of the square, waving her arms at me like she was carrying a flag in the Thicket High color guard. With a sigh, I detoured in that direction, and when we got close, Alana came around the table, twined her arm through Charlie's, and dragged him the rest of the way over.

"It's so good to see you again, Junior! And you're looking just *stunning* in that costume. I wonder... could you do me a teeny, tiny favor and stay at our table for, like, five minutes?" she begged, giving him the big, sad eyes that had melted all her ex-boyfriends into goo. In a lower voice, she added, "If you're here in your costume, everyone will come by and take Caroline's gourmet cranberry sauce. It's orange spice this year."

"It's Charlton," I interrupted gruffly. "He doesn't go by Junior anymore."

"Oh." Alana blinked at me, then blinked some more. "Yeah. Okay."

Charlie shot me a quick look I couldn't interpret before

turning and patting my sister's arm. "Of course, Alana. Happy to stick around, if it's okay with Hunter. I love an orange-spice cranberry sauce."

I snorted. "You would." Then I shrugged and added in a grumble, "Fine. But this doesn't count as part of the date."

Alana and Charlie *each* gave me a look this time, and both were easy to interpret. My sister's suggested I'd lost my mind, while Charlie's said he was close to laughter. I wasn't sure which was more irritating.

"What's got you so grumpy?" Alana demanded later when Charlie was deep in conversation with Caroline and a couple of older ladies about the pros and cons of using star anise—whatever that was—in cranberry sauce. "You got your reveng-apology at last, and Mom's already taken her shift and gone home to start baking, so she hasn't heard about how you're spending your date. You should be on cloud nine."

"I am," I insisted… grumpily. "I'm thrilled. Ecstatic. Fucking *overjoyed*. I'm just eager to leave, that's all. I have stuff to do."

"You want to get Charlton alone?" she teased, throwing in an eyebrow wiggle. "I guess Operation Turkey's working out, huh?"

Fortunately, Caroline called her away at that moment because I didn't know how to answer.

It had worked. Sort of. Except then, Dunn's little intervention had left me feeling like *I* was the villain in the piece, not the admitted turkeynapper in our midst. And if Dunn was right, then why the heck was I still so angry at Charlie? And if I was so angry, then why did the sight of the colorful feathers stretching across his ass make me want to pin him against the wall, rip that stupid costume off him, and kiss him until he screamed—

"I love the Stuffin'!" Charlie shook a jar of homemade cranberry sauce at me like a squelchy maraca. "I can't remember why I thought I didn't like this event. Everyone's been so kind, and Caroline's emailing me her family recipe, and—"

"Yeah, fine. Are we done?" I asked tersely. "Floor's not sanding itself."

"This is *your* date, as you keep reminding me, so if you say we're done, we're done." Charlie waved a magnanimous hand. "Go get me dirty."

No matter how hard I tried—and I definitely tried—I couldn't help but picture the sexy turkey all bare-muscled and covered in sweat and floor dust while low-tempo porn music played softly in the background.

Damn it.

"Hunter Jackson! You look like a man who wants some spicy sausage!" Marnie Partridge exclaimed, stepping into my personal space and snapping me out of my lurid daydream.

My face flooded with heat. "W-what? Me? *Heck no.* Definitely not."

"Oh." Marnie gave me a disappointed frown. "Well, that's too bad."

It took me a minute to notice she, Parrish, and Diesel were standing at the Partridge family table, handing out foil-covered sausage casseroles to anyone who walked by, and that Diesel was now glowering at me for snapping at his beloved aunt-in-law.

"Thanks anyway," Charlie said with an apologetic smile as we hurried away. "Smells great, but Hunter seems strangely sausage-averse at the moment."

I regretted my reaction after the scent of savory casserole hit my nose, but by then, we were well past the table. I sighed. "I should have gotten it. The Partridges make a killer casserole."

Charlie stopped, swiveled on his bird feet, and jogged back to the table to grab a foil pan. He flashed Parrish and Diesel's little daughter, Marigold, a charming smile before jogging back to me and shoving the pan at my chest. "Here."

I stared at him. "Why'd you do that?"

He shrugged, sending the arm feathers into a chaotic rustle. "Uh... because you wanted it?"

His simple explanation unsettled me. The cavalcade of stallions turned into a chaotic stampede. This wasn't at all what I'd planned when I'd pledged Brooks's money to last night's charity.

I made a throaty noise of generic—albeit confused—disapproval while wrapping my arms around the still-warm pan. "Thanks," I muttered.

"Not gonna lie, I also figured you might be hangry." Charlie grinned. "You used to get that way when we were kids. Remember that time we were swimming—"

"Not hangry," I interrupted, cutting off his stroll down happy-memory lane. "I'm just... focused. Thinking about the best way to sand the edges of the floor. You go *with* the grain. Keep that in mind."

Was it possible to sound more ridiculous? I doubted it.

When I got to the truck, I placed the casserole on the floor in the back seat and hopped in while Charlie wrestled himself into the passenger's side, almost leaning over my lap at one point to keep his tail feathers from getting caught in the door. The moment he got close, I forgot all about the aroma of the casserole because a swirl of some unidentifiable and far more enticing masculine scent filled the cab between us—a scent that was made up of comfortable, ordinary smells, like vanilla cookies and spicy whiskey and a woodstove in winter—making me crave something that definitely wasn't food. Suddenly, Charlie seemed very close... closer than he had on the way to town, even though the seats in my truck hadn't moved while the thing had been parked.

I fiddled with the blower as we got on the road, jacking up the heat in an attempt to calm myself down. "You must've been cold in that costume. I should've gotten you some sweatpants for under the tights."

"I'm okay. It's way colder in Chicago." He eased back in his seat, trying to get comfortable. "Besides, I've always run hot."

Not helping.

"Why Charlton?" I asked to distract myself from a large, possessive sniffing of his sexy-as-fuck cologne. "I mean, why were you and your father named that?"

"Oh." Charlie grinned. "After Charlton Heston, of course. You knew my grandfather, right? Ephron Nutter worshipped Charlton Heston as if the man were Moses himself." He cleared his throat and affected an exaggerated (and semi-familiar) Southern accent. "The 1956 *Ten Commandments* movie was the best damn production of all time! 'A city is built of brick, Pharoah. The strong make many, the starving make few. The dead make none.' You remember that, boy, when you think to treat someone unkindly. 'The dead make *none*.'" He shrugged and in his normal voice added, "I never really understood what it had to do with kindness, but whatever. It was enough to make him name my father after the man, along with Aunt Charli, Uncle Carl, and Uncle Hess. And then the name got passed down to me, plus a couple of cousins somewhere along the line. My grandfather had eight kids, so it's hard to keep track of everyone."

"You're telling me half a generation of Nutters, plus more in your generation, got named after Charlton Heston because... Moses didn't agree with killing slaves? That might be the most small-town Tennessee bullshit I've ever heard, and I've lived in the Thicket my whole life."

The turkey lifted an eyebrow at me. "Are you implying that Grandaddy Nutter had a screw loose?"

It took me a second to notice the corner of his lip was curved up. "Maybe. The apple doesn't fall far from the tree."

Charlie snorted. "Why do you think I wanted to get the hell out of here as soon as possible?" His almost-grin disappeared. "I worried I'd become... just another Nutter."

"Hey, now. Your family are good people," I defended automatically, and I meant it. Other than Charlie's father, the Nutters had been part of the bedrock of the town for generations. They were one of those families always willing to lend a hand to help a neighbor in need. They were a little quirky, even by Thicket standards, but they were also dependable, honest, and hard-working.

"I know." Charlie ran long fingers through his hair and turned away to look out the truck window, absorbed by his own thoughts. "At least when they're not teasing me and poking their nose into my business until I lose my mind."

"Pfft. That's what family *does*, whether it's the family you're born into or the family you make for yourself along the way."

As we turned onto my parents' property and headed up the bumpy gravel drive toward the barn, I noticed a haphazard pile of paint cans in front of the door beneath a smattering of half-dried, splotchy green swatches that made the old wood look like a seasick giraffe.

I sighed. Alana had probably been too impatient to wait

until Friday to pick a paint color, and I'd bet my whole business that none of the paintbrushes had been cleaned.

"Sometimes seems like it's my family's entire job to make me lose my mind," I admitted. "And that's without the stress of the holidays in the mix. But..." I hesitated. I'd never found it easy to express my deepest thoughts, and I grasped for the right words. "Even so, I wouldn't trade them for anything. Loving folks means accepting them as they are, I figure—good and bad, annoying and wonderful—the same way you want them to accept you. They're loud and interfering sometimes, and you might not enjoy every minute of their company, but they're *yours*, and you're *theirs*. Remembering that helps you take the bad with the good." I scratched at my beard. "Or at least that's how I think about it."

Charlie looked at me and nodded seriously, like he'd been listening hard and thought I'd said something profound.

After everything else that day—the angry banter, the smirky looks, the improbably sexy turkey costume, the bewildered but genuine smile on his face while he chatted with random Thicketeers—that simple, serious nod felt like it might be my undoing. The uncomfortable feeling in my belly returned a thousandfold, and I wanted nothing more than to get away from Charlie before I did something unforgivably stupid... like pulling him close.

When I pulled up next to the side-by-side he'd driven over from Amos's place, I found myself saying in a rare burst of charity, "You don't need to stay. I'll sand the floor. You're..." I gestured to his grand be-featherment. "You're all paid up."

He stared at me, but it was hard to tell if it was in relief or consternation. "Explain."

Instead of explaining or spending any more moments closed inside the small truck cab that now smelled like sexy man on turkey steroids, I opened the door and hopped out. "We're good," I called over my shoulder before slamming the door behind me. "Fly free, little bird."

Charlie climbed out his side and came around to face me. When he put his hands on his hips, the orange feather fans jutted out to each side. "What, so you can complain fifteen years from now that I *stole* an extra hour from you or that I'm lazy?" He jutted his chin out. "No way. You paid for four hours, you get four hours."

I clutched my keys in tense fingers and strode past him toward the barn. "Time off for good behavior. Turkeys get pardoned the day before Thanksgiving. Go be with your family. Eat some of your gross cranberry sauce."

But the crunch of his booted turkey feet followed me into the cavernous space.

"Wow, this looks amazing," he said, completely ignoring my call for his immediate departure. "You said Alana's turning it into an event space? A wedding here would be beautiful."

I looked around, trying to see the old space through new eyes while unobtrusively moving as far away from Charlie as I could. "Yeah. Alana actually got the idea after hearing that Marissa Drakes had a hard time finding a nice place to get married in the Thicket. Plus, the community center barn is the only large indoor gathering space in town, and you can imagine that's booked up most of the time, what with all the town celebrations, so there's a real need for a second venue to host non-wedding events too." I was babbling but couldn't stop myself. "When Alana was at school in Memphis, she had a job working events at a hotel downtown, and later, she worked as a waitress here in town, so she knows lots about planning functions. Just seemed like a natural fit."

Charlie walked around, peering into doorways and checking out the built-in bars along one side. I couldn't help but chart exactly how many paces separated us at any given moment. "Have you talked to Quinn Taffet about your plans? He'd be all over this." Charlie glanced over at me. "I met him last night at the auction. Seems like a sweetheart."

"He's taken," I blurted. "And his husband is a big guy. The biggest. Ex-military type named Percy Champion. You don't want to mess with Champ."

"Uh." Charlie's eyes went wide with surprise. "I was talking to Quinn for like... a minute? I wasn't propositioning him. It was mostly small talk about Chicago weddings while we waited to be presented onstage."

My cheeks felt like molten lava. "No, I'm sure. I just meant..."

He lifted an eyebrow at me. "Meant...?"

I waved a hand vaguely through the air. "Meant that, yes, Quinn knows about Alana's plans."

"Right." Charlie studied me, which only made the lava on my cheeks hotter. "Are you okay? You seem jumpy."

"Jumpy? Me? Pfft. I'm the opposite of jumpy. I'm... I'm still." I bent my knees a little to make my feet even more like cement blocks than they already were and pointed down to my feet. "See?"

The turkey twisted his tongue in his mouth like he was trying not to laugh.

I glared at him. "You can go now."

"No. You challenged my work ethic last night, and I won't back down from a challenge. I think I'm going to take a turn with this puppy." He nodded toward the industrial sander before wandering over to it and plugging it into the nearest outlet. He made such a ridiculous picture—a turkey-man preparing to work a large metal power sander—that I couldn't even bring myself to tell him that we didn't need the machine for the work we were doing today. Instead, I pulled out my phone and snapped a few quick pictures before I could think better of it.

"What are you doing?" he asked, catching me mid-snap.

"I... nothing."

Charlie looked down at the costume he still wore. "Oh. Right. I guess I should probably take this off." He let go of the sander and yanked at the tie that held his headpiece in place, then knelt to remove his turkey feet. When he straightened, his muscles flexed against the fabric of his costume, making it clear that he wasn't wearing anything beneath.

"No! No. That's... not necessary," I said as the stallion stampede galloped around my gut. "Truly. In fact, if you're determined to stay and work, I think it makes sense to keep the costume on. For, you know... protection."

But even as I said the words, other parts of my anatomy were sending up their own silent plea. *Please, baby Moses in all of your slave-based wisdom, let this man sand my floors in his turkey costume.*

Naturally, the plea I didn't want him to hear was the one the contrary man responded to. With a quick eye roll that let me know what he thought about my idea of "protection," he reached up and grasped the zipper pull on the front of his costume.

And then, in achingly slow motion, like something out of a *very* niche-kink porn video, the sexy turkey yanked down the zipper... and stripped off all his feathers.

Chapter Five

Charlton

Hunter was staring at me again.

I'd only intended to save the bulk of the turkey costume from the inevitable sanding dust. But after I'd unzipped the top portion, Hunter's eyes had gone hot and glassy, and the tip of his tongue had darted out to lick his lips in a way that made me freeze in place and pray my dick would do the same.

Suddenly, I remembered my conversation with Seamus about refinishing floors and double entendres and wondered if he'd been right all along. Maybe Hunter, my former friend and current semi-enemy, was more interested in the other kind of *floor refinishing* than in doing actual renovation work.

And wouldn't that be the most unexpected development in a week of unprecedented surprises?

Hunter had been driving me crazy all morning. The man was ten tons of snark packed into six-plus feet of muscular farmer, which was my personal kryptonite. Not to mention, he smelled like clean sweat, hay, and maple syrup, which I would never have imagined was a lust-inducing combo, but for some reason was really doing it for me. If the man kept staring, things were about to get very physical in a way neither one of us had anticipated.

I mean, not to say I'd never thought about Hunter that way. I definitely *had*. Skinny, virginal, teenage me had spent hours and hours thinking about his generous lips and his powerful muscles, even before I'd known exactly what I'd want those lips and muscles to do to me. And last night, under cover of darkness in Amos's bunk room, I'd thought about Hunter again... this time in much greater detail.

But those had been fantasies. The reality was my time today had been bought and paid for—and not in a sexual way, despite anyone's ideas to the contrary. Which meant I needed to strip my costume without making it seem like I was, you know... *stripping my costume.*

I grasped for some way to distract us both, and what came out of my mouth was, "You know, you never told me how Dolly Parton got his name."

"Huh?" The reminder of his supposed "prize" turkey snapped Hunter out of the tongue thing. "Oh, that. It... uh..." His cheeks went pink, and he scratched the back of his neck in an obvious tell. "Who even remembers?"

I tilted my head, genuinely curious now. "About every-thing concerning that turkey? You. Definitely you."

Hunter dropped his hands to his sides. "Fine, then. Not like it matters anymore anyway. I, ah, got Dolly as a poult from a heritage breeder over in Great Nuthatch right around Labor Day, and I was showing him off at our family cookout. My cousin Kelsey—she was, like, three at the time—thought he was the cutest thing, puffing out his feathers and chirping all over the place. She said he sounded like..." He cleared his throat. "Like Dolly Parton."

"Oh my God." I pressed a hand to my bare chest. "That's adorable."

"Yeah, well. My uncle Clem didn't think so," Hunter said grimly. "Told her to stop being silly because that poult was a tom, not a hen, and it had to have a boy name. Kelsey bawled, and that got everyone riled—she's my mom's favorite niece, you know?—and I told Clem that it didn't matter if the bird was male or female, it was *my* choice, and a bird as majestic as mine should be named for the most majestic sight in all of Tennessee." He shrugged. "So, we christened him Dolly Parton. And later, Clem agreed that the turkey had a magnificent bosom. So."

I laughed out loud, and he shot me a disgruntled look.

"Yeah, yeah, laugh it up. But you should know that poor little Kelsey was *devastated* when she heard about Dolly's violent, horrific assault a few months later at the hands of someone Dolly thought was his friend."

My laughter evaporated, and my back teeth ground together. "Oh, for fuck's sake. There was no assault, Hunter, violent or otherwise! I put the damned bird in a pillowcase and treated it like the prince you thought he—wait," I said as I belatedly recognized the name he'd mentioned. "*Wait.* Are you talking about Kelsey Jackson? The one who owns the boxing gym in town? The one who bid on Jim McNeely last night for the sole purpose of, and I quote, 'fucking him up' in the ring? *She's* poor little Kelsey?"

Hunter sniffed and inspected his fingernails. "What can I say? Early childhood trauma has devastating effects."

Jesus. Why was I so damned attracted to this smart-ass? He was hot as hell and annoying as fuck, but somehow, being annoying just made him hotter. I imagined putting my hand over his face to shut him up while sinking to my knees to suck him off.

Maybe there was something wrong with me. Maybe the tight turkey costume had cut off blood flow to my brain. Or maybe my brain had been scrambled since the first time I'd looked at Hunter, back when we were kids, and thought, *"Yes. Him."*

"Whatever. Let's finish this." I took a step away and peeled the costume off, leaving me bare to the waist. The cold air inside the cavernous barn hit the skin of my arms and chest, making me shiver... and reminding me I'd left my jeans, shirt, and hoodie in the side-by-side I'd borrowed from my uncle to drive over here this morning. "Ideally before I freeze to death. Would you mind getting my clothes out of the side-by-side?"

But Hunter didn't move. His eyes were as wide as I'd ever seen them as he stared at my brown-tights-covered... *giblets*... which only served to make them mutually interested in his gaze.

"You're wearing tights," he said in a squeaky voice.

I dropped my hands down to cover myself. "Obviously! You're the one who gave me this costume. If I hadn't worn the tights, my legs *would* have frozen off."

The heat of his gaze seared my ass, and a strange noise escaped his throat. "But you're *only* wearing... and there isn't... I can practically see your..."

"My clothes, please?" I huffed impatiently. "Anytime you're ready."

Once again, he didn't respond, but this time, the sound of his boot heels striking the bare wood floor indicated his agreement. I waited for his return, trying not to shiver in the November air. When my clothes landed in a pile on the floor in front of me, I wanted to turn and scowl. Instead, I made a production of leaning over and displaying my ass in as sexy a way as stripping off thick brown tights would allow. When another strangled noise escaped his throat, I hid a smug grin.

Take that, turkey-freak.

As soon as I had my clothes on, I turned around in time to catch sight of Hunter's ruddy cheeks. Knowing he was at least a little bit affected by me despite his anger was gratifying. It was nice not to be the only one in this predicament.

When he caught me looking, Hunter coughed and immediately became engrossed in the giant industrial sander, flipping switches and turning dials on the controls with all the frowning concentration of a man attempting a lunar landing.

"You do know how to use this, right?" I asked once he'd flipped the same switch off and on three times.

He glanced up at me, blinked, and then looked back down at the sander like he wasn't sure how it had gotten there or why he'd been touching it. Then he frowned again and reached down to unplug it while his face went even redder.

"Uh. Floor refinishing novice here." I hooked a thumb at my own chest. "But I think you need electricity to make it work."

"Thank you, genius, but we're not using this machine," he said without looking at me. "Most of the floor's already sanded. What's left are all the edges and fiddly bits where the machine can't reach. Those need to be sanded by hand."

I looked at the giant space, this time noticing how many corners, columns, pipes, and other obstructions stuck out of the floor. The majority of the wood was a dull, grayish-white, but a two-inch border around each obstruction was dark with dirt and age.

I groaned. No wonder Hunter was willing to pay two grand to get a sucker to help do the job. "Do you have a cushion I can use? It's the least you could do if you want me to spend an hour on my knees for you."

My comment had been totally innocent, but when it made Hunter's blush turn a truly concerning shade of red, I quickly realized how he'd interpreted it.

Before I could open my mouth to correct myself, he strode over to a folding table that held random piles of supplies and equipment before returning with a pair of knee pads and a cordless palm sander. He held them out to me, still not meeting my gaze. "Use these," he said gruffly. "There are extra batteries on the table."

I stared after him as he returned to the table to get his own pair of knee pads and palm sander. I'd never wanted to pick a fight as badly as I did right then, if only to make him look at me. A thousand snarky comments piled up behind my teeth, and my hands gripped the sander way tighter than necessary. But then I imagined my mother raving about the Waldorf's cucumber water if Hunter "Bird-Obsessed" Jackson let it slip that I'd spent my afternoon fighting instead of working, and I managed to hold myself back.

Fortunately, we got down to business after that, and for a long while, I was too focused on refinishing Hunter's floor to worry about *refinishing Hunter's—no*. I needed to stop thinking in double entendres immediately. Giving in would mean I'd fully re-assimilated into the Thicket, and I was not here for that—I was too focused on refinishing the floor to worry about *anything*, and that was a nice change. My muscles warmed and loosened, and the damp heat of sweat beaded against my skin until I had to pull off my hoodie.

The physical work was far from my daily routine, which usually involved toiling at my desk sending emails or meeting with other executives about projection spread-sheets. Recently, my boss had dumped so many projects in my lap that I'd told Seamus I felt like I was standing beside a problem conveyor belt, with barely enough time to solve one problem before the next was in front of me. I certainly never got a chance to see the fruits of my labor in a meaningful way, the way you could with floor sanding.

But while that was often frustrating, I reminded myself that every job had its downsides. My career was stable, and the work itself was mentally stimulating—logistics was like a puzzle, and I'd always been good at those—plus, all the hours spent at work meant even my matchmaking mother couldn't nag me to date more. At least, not as much as she'd probably like to.

A bottle of water dripping with condensation rolled toward me and bumped into the side of my knee, jolting me out of my justifications. I looked up from the pipe I was sanding around and turned off the palm sander when I saw Hunter cracking open his own bottle of water.

"Drink that," he said gruffly, nodding at my bottle. "You've been working up a sweat."

So had Hunter. The front of his shirt was plastered to his chest and shoulders, highlighting every ripple of muscle. *This is what he'd look like in bed*, I thought helplessly. *This is what he'd look like after we'd worked up a sweat in a different way.*

I looked away quickly. *Fantasy, not reality*, I reminded myself.

I flipped over to sit down and uncapped the water before taking a deep sip. "Thanks."

"You do good work, Nutter. Better than I thought," he said, like his honor compelled him to admit it, and I couldn't deny the warm rush of pleasure at the grudging compliment.

"I'm not lazy," I reminded him. "Never was. Remember

how I earned that skating merit badge one bruising fall at a time?"

Hunter's lips twitched. "I remember since I was the guy you were falling on most of the time. But I wasn't sure if you'd be up for this sort of work, what with you being a corporate drudge and all."

There wasn't a direct question there, but Hunter set his water bottle in the center of the floor and dropped down beside it, draping his elbows over his bent knees, and regarded me curiously anyway.

"Yeah, well." I wiped my mouth with the back of my forearm. "I do spend my day behind a desk, but even us corporate drudges hit the gym occasionally."

Hunter looked me up and down for a moment as if measuring my physique to determine the truth of my words, then muttered a noncommittal "mmm."

"*Mmm?*" I repeated, scowling. "What's that supposed to mean? I have a gym membership. I work out." I wasn't built on the same scale as Hunter, but I was plenty strong. I casually flexed my biceps, hoping they'd show to good effect under my own sweat-damp T-shirt.

"Meh." Hunter shrugged. "I've heard about those city gyms. You ride a Peloton while discussing stock prices with your fellow city-folk, right?"

I opened my mouth to disagree, then remembered my most recent spin class and closed it again. "I lift weights too," I said, chin in the air.

"Sure, I can see that," he agreed. "*Paper*weights, I assume?"

I made a noise of outrage, and Hunter burst into laughter that made it clear he'd been teasing... and I'd given him exactly the reaction he'd wanted.

"Nobody uses *paper* anymore. Jesus," I said in the most

dignified voice I could muster. "And besides, we can't all be muscle-bound, uh..." I racked my brain for the few snippets of information about Hunter that my cousins had let slip the night before. "Plant farmers?"

His smile widened. "I prefer nursery owner. I started Jackson's Organic Blooms after I came back from college."

"You started your own business? Here in the Thicket? How'd you decide on that?" I wondered.

Hunter scratched his beard and shrugged. "The usual way, I guess. I've always loved farm life, measuring time by the way things grow."

I nodded. I remembered this about him.

"I started growing plants in high school, so that was kind of a natural fit, and I knew I didn't want to work for anyone else." He placed one elbow behind his head and pushed it down with the opposite hand, wincing at the stretch. "And Licking Thicket's my home. So I told my parents my plans and convinced them to let me set up my greenhouses on a parcel of their land. Took a couple years, but things are going well."

I nodded. "Good for you. Lucky everything worked out like that."

"Lucky?" Hunter narrowed his eyes. "Hardly. I appreciate what my parents did, don't get me wrong, but it wasn't *luck* that made the business a success."

I realized I'd misspoken, but before I could jump in to explain or apologize and defuse the situation, Hunter had already begun speaking again, ticking items off on his fingers defensively. "The first couple years, I did *everything* myself. Planted every seed, then loaded up the truck and sold plants directly to locals at farmer's markets and the like. There's a lot of demand for organic houseplants—especially the kind I focus on, which aren't toxic to pets—

so I kept building the business year after year. I kept reinvesting my earnings. Now, I have five full-time employees, and we still run a booth at the Thicket market every summer Friday just to keep a hand in, but the bulk of our business comes from floral shops and garden centers. We're one of the biggest plant suppliers in Middle Tennessee... so far." He blew out a breath like he was calming himself down. "There's more opportunity in the Thicket than you might think, but you don't need *luck* to find it. You just need to be committed to staying and willing to work hard."

The last part of this statement felt like criticism, and suddenly, I was feeling defensive too. "I just meant you're *lucky* that your dreams were a good match for the Thicket, that's all," I explained. "It'd be pretty hard to be an astronaut here. Or an artist since there are no galleries. Or some Silicon Valley–type technology inventor."

Hunter huffed out a laugh. "You think?"

"I know," I said firmly. "I'm not trying to take anything away from what you've done, because it's amazing. *It is.* But it wouldn't work for everyone or even most people."

"You're not close to your cousin Buck, are you?"

I had no idea what one thing had to do with the other. "Not really," I admitted. "He's from the Grapeseed branch of the family—Grapeseed was Uncle Amos's brother, just like my grandfather Ephron—and they're a little offbeat, even for Nutters." I frowned. "Why do you ask?"

"Oh... no reason," he said airily, though the smirk on his face said he knew something I didn't. He stretched out one leg so that his booted foot was mere inches from my ankle and gave me an assessing look. "So what is it *you* do, exactly? Town rumors only say you've got a fancy title and you make rock-star money, but I'm not sure which rock star they mean. Are we talking Beyoncé? Or Willie Nelson after the IRS got him?"

A startled burst of laughter escaped me. "Somewhere in between? I'm the vice president of distribution and logistics for one of the largest industrial kitchen supply companies in the Midwest," I said with a little tinge of pride. When Hunter's brow furrowed, I explained, "Distribution means I oversee the movement of supplies from one place to another. From the manufacturer to a warehouse sometimes, or from the warehouse to the clients."

"Ohhhh. Is *that* what distribution means? I get it now." Hunter tucked his tongue into his cheek. "You sell pots and pans, like down at the Cozy Kitchen, but for professionals."

I was distracted by the way golden afternoon light spilling through the window glinted off his beard, and for a moment, I couldn't process what he was saying. "No. I-I mean, yes. I mean... I don't do the selling. I, ah... I move the stuff around after it's sold?"

"Ah, so more like a truck driver!" He nodded aggressively. "Gotcha, gotcha. My uncle Pete was a long-hauler for a while. That's lonely work, buddy—"

"*Not* like a trucker," I snapped. "I manage the people who coordinate the transportation. Sometimes it's trucking, or cargo ships, or freight trains, or expedited aviation. The options are endless, depending on the parameters of the client's budget and the urgency of the, ah... need," I finished in a small voice. It sounded kind of pathetic when I described it out loud.

And the laughing gleam in Hunter's eyes said he'd been teasing me.

Again.

"Fuck off," I muttered, kicking his foot.

"Sorry, sorry. I couldn't resist," Hunter said, holding up

his hands in surrender. "You were just so earnest about the '*distribution means*' thing." He rubbed his palms against his thighs. "Seriously, though, you're in distribution, managing coordinators who send the stuff to... other places. But do you at least get to try out the stuff? Do you believe in the company? Are the products good?"

"I assume so. I've never seen any of it before. I don't work at the warehouse, and they don't give out samples. And, well, I don't cook much anyway." I pulled at the neck of my T-shirt distractedly.

"No?" Hunter gave me a soft smile that did things to my stomach. "Well, as long as you know the clients like it, I guess."

"Yeah. I mean... They must like it, right? They keep ordering, and my team keeps shipping them stuff."

"So, you don't really get to talk to the people who make the products *or* the people who use them? And you don't know if you like the stuff you're moving around or if the people who get the stuff are happy? You just deal with the problems in the middle?" He wrinkled his nose. "And you... like that?"

He didn't sound judgmental so much as bewildered, but I felt judged all the same... maybe because his honest appraisal of my job knocked down the little wall of justifications I'd been building in my mind.

"Yes, I do." I scrambled to my knees. "I mean, would I like to have face time with actual clients? Yeah. And to feel like I wasn't just a... a cog in a machine? Sure. But you know what else I like? Affording rent, and food, and 401k contributions, and supplementing my mother's spa habit. My dad gave me school money, but I'm not independently wealthy. I live in the real world, and not every job is perfect, okay?"

"Whoa, whoa, what are you getting angry for?" Hunter

demanded, pushing to his feet. "It's just... back when I knew you, you were all about making connections with people. First kid on the volunteer list when Old Mr. Dixon's yard needed mowed the summer we were twelve, the kid who spent his whole recess comforting Petey Van Sant after Ms. Wolf teased him for not being able to pronounce Newfoundland in fourth grade. That was why I liked you so—" He caught himself and broke off with a fierce frown. "I mean, that was why it pissed me off when you betrayed me!"

The sigh I emitted sounded more like a feral growl, and I jumped to my feet too, needing to put us on equal footing. "Oh, for goodness' sake, not this again—"

"But I guess you weren't that person to begin with, were you?" Hunter pushed on, as heated as I was. "You wanted to leave the Thicket and be a big success, right? Well, congratulations. You got what you wanted." He folded his arms across his chest and added in a mutter, "Though it sounds hella boring, not gonna lie."

I sucked in a deep, angry breath. Why was I letting this man get in my head and make me question things? I had a stable career I enjoyed and a job at a company I... didn't hate. I was making a name for myself, supporting *myself*, which was more than my father had ever done, damn it. And if Hunter didn't understand that, then fuck him.

I should have taken the out he'd offered me earlier and gone home, if only to avoid his incessant judging. What did I care if he thought I was lazy? No niceness bet was worth this.

I stepped closer to him and leaned in his face. "Well, I don't care what you think. I graduated with honors from U of I in Logistics and Supply Chain Management. I was recruited into one of the top logistics programs in Chicago. I worked my ass off to get promoted to vice president, and yes, I'm proud of it. I move billions of tiny pieces around a giant game board in my mind to make sure things get where they need to be when they need to be there, and without people like me and my team, business owners like *you* wouldn't be able to share their products with the world. It's important work. And I don't need a fucking *nursery owner* making me feel like I work the graveyard shift at a... a... a *daylight factory!*"

I broke off to stare at Hunter, my breath heaving. I played back my own words and was pretty sure I wasn't making sense anymore, if I ever had been.

Sweat-drenched with turkey-hat hair and coated in sawdust, I probably looked like a homicidal powdered donut, deranged and out of control. Hell, I felt out of control, like I was riding the Hunter roller coaster again, but this time, the ride was on fire. It was curiously freeing, though, letting myself feel my feelings without holding back.

"I'm here on my damned hands and knees, sanding a barn floor for you," I went on because I was on a roll. "And you..."

My voice trailed off as I realized that while I was speaking, Hunter's gaze had glued itself to my lips. The temperature in the room ratcheted up several degrees, and my skin blazed with heat that had nothing to do with hard work or even anger...

And everything to do with his hot stare.

"Y-you..." I licked my lips and tried again. "You..."

Hunter's eyes bored into me until I couldn't stand it anymore—which, admittedly, probably took all of half a second. Like earlier, he didn't move, didn't try to touch me, yet my lips felt like they were being branded. My head swam with an intense combination of anger, confusion, and base desire until the sole focus of my being became the movement of his lips just inches from mine and that ever-present heat in his gaze... and the moment I stopped trying to convince myself that frustrating, provoking, stubborn-as-fuck Hunter Jackson was the last person I should want, I was lost.

So I did what I should have done the moment Hunter raised his damn paddle and bid his way back into my life.

"Ah, fuck it," I muttered. Then I fisted the front of his shirt, yanked him close, and shut him up with my mouth.

Our lips crashed together, and something inside of me let out an epic sigh of relief. *Here. Finally. The man's mouth is exactly where it should be.*

And just like that, all of the anger that had been burning me up transmuted itself into a desperate passion that was no less hot but a whole hell of a lot more honest than our bickering had been.

At first, Hunter grappled with me, and I had a moment's panic that I'd misread the signs, that he didn't want me at all. But as soon as I tried to pull back, he grabbed my head and held it tightly, deepening the kiss and grumbling into my mouth with a wordless warning not to pull away, not to stop a kiss I didn't want to end in the first place.

I grabbed him around his waist, dragging him even closer as if I could make our bodies merge into a solid block of never-stop. As I moved a hand down to grab his ass, I wondered fleetingly if this would earn me extra credit points in my mother's niceness bet.

Because this hot encounter with Hunter Jackson was one of the *nicest* things I'd experienced in a long, long time.

Chapter Six

Hunter

CHARLIE'S KISS was so fucking wild, so feral, so exactly what I'd been craving, I didn't care how foolish and short-sighted I was being. I needed more.

So, I did what any hot-blooded gay man would do when faced with the sexy, riled-up turkey who'd invaded his brain.

"Let me suck you off," I begged, gasping between kisses. "Please, Charlie. Fuck."

Charlie grunted an enthusiastic agreement and moved his hands to his fly, and I decided to help by moving my hands to the delectable ass that had been taunting me for... Jesus, had it really only been a day? It felt like way longer. Like *forever*.

I'd barely managed an appreciative squeeze of the thick muscle—really, more people should consider adding Peloton and paperweights to their gym routines, if this kind of glory was the result—and allowed a single tortured groan to slide out of my throat before the sound of Morgan Waller's "Last Night" playing at top volume pierced the air, followed by the crunch of gravel as someone braked to a hard stop on the gravel driveway just outside the barn.

In the space of a single gasping breath, Charlie and I sprang apart from each other like we were still kids who'd gotten caught with our hands in a cookie jar.

Thinking about Charlie's cookie jar was only going to make the situation worse, so instead, I fixed him with a hard look. "Nothing happened," I hissed in warning.

His forehead crinkled, and his kiss-swollen lips pursed in confusion. "As in, it didn't happen *yet*, but you'd like it to? Or as in, you're denying the fact it was absolutely *going* to happen if we hadn't been interrupted? Because—"

I threw up my hands and cut him off with a whispered, "Either! Both. I don't know! Just stop talking about it, okay?"

Charlie's eyes widened at my reaction, and I could hardly blame him.

I'd been just as into that kiss as he had, but I also knew that whoever was approaching the barn—probably someone from my family, and please, baby Jesus, not my mother— would freak right the fuck out if they knew what he and I had been up to. At a minimum, I'd be teased about getting caught on my "date" with Junior Nutter for the rest of my born days, long after the man left the Thicket. At worst, my mother would decide hooking up with him was a cry for help.

Charlie glanced behind me to make sure no one had entered yet before narrowing his eyes and lowering his voice. "Don't tell me you didn't want it."

I opened my mouth to say exactly that, but the lie wouldn't come off my tongue.

His frown turned into a knowing grin as my sister's distinctive speed-walking pace hit the hardwood floor. "I'll be back tonight." He met my eyes, and I felt the burn deep in my gut. "To finish what we started."

As he turned and made his way out of the barn, exchanging polite greetings with Alana, I stared after him.

Was that a threat or a promise?

My dick throbbed in horny confusion. I tried desperately to change the direction of my thoughts before my sister got close enough for an awkward encounter. Thankfully, the sound of Charlie slamming the door to his side-by-side jerked me out of my haze.

He was angry again, and I wasn't sure whether it was because we'd kissed... or because we'd been interrupted.

"Hey. What brings you by?" I asked my sister, sounding as casual as a man could when ninety-nine percent of his blood supply refused to circulate above his waist. "Come to see how your paint swatches dried? Or did you want to make sure I wasn't mistreating the turkey?"

"Hmm?" Alana tossed her designer handbag onto the dusty worktable by the door, her attention still focused on Charlie, who'd fired up the engine on the side-by-side. "Oh. Neither. I told Mom I'd help her bake desserts this afternoon." She gave a curled-finger wave in Charlie's direction before turning toward me with a dramatic sigh. "Good gravy. That man is hot as hell and a total sweetie pie to boot." She sighed again. "Too bad he's gay."

As the words trailed off, she seemed to realize that she knew an eligible gay man who should be benefitting from this situation, and her eyebrows rose to her hairline. "Speaking of which—"

"No," I barked. "Don't say it. Do not—"

"—now that your date is over and your feud is finished, you should totally hit that!"

"Nobody uses that phrase anymore," I said desperately.

"Besides, you heard what I said last night. Charlie is persona non grata—"

"Oh, I heard alright," Alana agreed, stalking closer and using her laser-eye-contact power on me, though I tried valiantly to put up my shields. "But that was before you went and spent two *thousand* dollars on the man, then paraded him around the town square."

"Nothing's changed," I insisted, not sure which of us I was trying to convince anymore. "He stole—"

"If you mention Dolly Parton again, I'm going to get violent." Alana set her hands on her hips. "You know how much I loved that turkey. I treated him like my own personal baby doll whenever I could get away with it. Remember how annoyed you'd get when you caught me making him flower necklaces and putting him in my doll carriage? And even *I* think you're being ridiculous. Charlton didn't hurt Dolly. He brought him home safe and sound. Heck, he'd given the bird a bath."

"Even so."

This comment provoked a withering look I was pretty sure I deserved. "You're just looking for excuses, aren't you? I know that three-quarters of your personality is pure stubbornness, Hunter, and most of the time, that's a good thing. It led you to build a huge, thriving business when other folks might've settled for good enough. Keeps Mom from setting you up with a different man every day of the week and two on Sunday. It makes you take on huge jobs—" She waved a hand to indicate the barn renovation. "—even if it means learning as you go. But stubborn as you are, it's not like you to be closed-minded. Or mean. Or angry at someone who wasn't much older than little Jack Nutter when this incident happened. So what gives?"

"I... I don't know," I admitted, running a hand over my

face. I was confused by my own feelings. Hell, I was confused to find I had feelings at all. Two days ago, I'd have told anyone with perfect sincerity that I hadn't thought of Junior Nutter in years, and now... Now I wondered if all along he'd been like the gap in my mouth after I'd had a tooth knocked out in Little League—an empty spot where something used to be, a bruise I couldn't stop pressing.

When Charlie had reappeared, my first instinct had been to remind everyone of the bad things he'd done. Turkeynapping. Friendship-betraying. Abandoning me—I mean, *everyone* in the Thicket—for his fancy life. I'd been provoking and defensive. I'd been grumpy. I'd wanted to teach him a lesson.

But with every one of his sweet smiles and eye rolls, every sexy turkey twerk and impassioned conversation about his career, every hour watching him sand my floor with tongue-between-his-teeth concentration, and every riled-up, mind-melting kiss, the person learning their lesson was *me*.

No matter what happened during The Great Turkey Incident fifteen years ago, the Charlie Nutter of today was a good person. A person I could like. A person I wanted.

Badly.

"Look, just hear me out," Alana went on. "Why not have a holiday fling with the hot turkey?"

Her statement so closely aligned with my own thoughts that I fumbled the scraps of used sandpaper I'd been collecting from the floor. "Wha—? No. We're not talking about this, Alana."

"A long weekend is the optimal length of time for a fling. He'll be gone before Mom can get any ideas in her head—"

I shot her a disbelieving look. Our mother could go from

zero to sixty ideas in under a second, faster than a luxury sports car.

"Before she can *act* on them, then," Alana corrected. "And since he probably won't be back anytime soon, there'll be no tricky relationship entanglements. You should go after him now, Hunter. Today. Go pluck that bird!"

The reminder that Charlie might disappear again for another fifteen years soured my stomach. I kicked one of the sandpaper balls. "Classy, but no. I don't like meaningless *plucks*. You know that."

With the taste of Charlie's kiss still in my mouth, the words felt a bit like a lie. I *did* eventually want a committed relationship. And I truly *didn't* like hookups in general, but I couldn't deny that I'd make an exception for Charlie Nutter if given the opportunity. *I wouldn't kick him outta bed for eating crackers.*

And then what?

There was no world in which a career-focused city boy like Charlie Nutter, with his important executive job and fancy suits, would ever want more than a quick hookup with a workaholic Thicket farmer. And part of the reason I avoided hookups was because my own steady (*stubborn*, Alana's voice corrected in my head) nature made it way too easy for me to get attached.

Imagining myself falling for a man who was a couple of hundred miles from me geographically and a million light-years away in lifestyle felt like willingly walking into a nightmare. And if the Thicket gossips ever heard about our hookup, I'd be living that nightmare forever, like my own terrible *Groundhog Day*.

"I appreciate your concern. I do. But I've got all the fun I want right here." I swept my arms out to indicate the half-finished space around us. "Besides, I have plans this afternoon. I was thinking I might crash your dessert baking," I said, making the decision as I spoke. Keeping busy was the best way to stop myself from doing anything foolish...

Or anything *more* foolish than I'd already done.

"You're *voluntarily* spending time with Mom right after your date?" Alana demanded. "Are you being brave or stupid? I can't tell."

"Neither." I waved away her concern. "I'm spending time with my beloved family. Mom will be too busy baking to bother me much, and if she asks about this morning, I'll tell her the same thing I'm telling you: I bid on a date with Charlie Nutter, and now it's done. End of story."

Alana's look said she didn't believe me—fair enough, since Charlie's *I'll be back tonight* was still playing on a loop in my head—but she dropped the subject anyway.

We finished cleaning up the sandpaper and abandoned paintbrushes, and as we walked over to our parents' house, we discussed the extensive list of desserts that our extended family had requested for the next day's feast.

"Eight pies and a crumble, kids!" our mother greeted as we walked in the back door. She had her sleeves rolled up and was elbows-deep in a giant bowl of what appeared to be sugar and butter while abandoned measuring cups cluttered the huge worktop and flour coated her apron, but her eyeliner still looked sharp, and her smile was triumphant.

There was nothing Lurleen Jackson loved more than feeding her extended family, which meant preparing our Thanksgiving feast was her personal Super Bowl—equal parts stressful and thrilling.

"I've already done the banana pudding, the pecan pie, the chocolate pecan pie, and the chocolate-*not*-pecan pie," she went on before either of us could say a single word, "but the cornucopia cookies need frosting, the cranberry filling is missing its crumble topping, and I need enough apples for four of my deep-dish apple pies." When neither of us immediately sprang into action, she removed one buttery hand from the bowl and waved imperiously. "Are you waiting for an invitation? This crumble ain't gonna crumble itself. Wash those hands, people."

Alana and I exchanged a look and hurried to the sink like we were still eight-year-olds, jockeying for position.

"How much coffee do you think she's had?" Alana demanded in a whisper.

I snorted. "Too much."

"And Hunter Jackson, once we've got these desserts in the oven, I wanna talk *alllll* about your date with that sweet Nutter boy," my mother called over her shoulder.

"Or possibly not enough," I muttered.

Because Alana was the best sister ever, before we began fetching, chopping, and peeling at our mother's direction, she pulled a portable speaker from her purse and cued up a playlist of classic pop hits. For a long while, we were all so busy singing along and occasionally arguing over what constituted a classic—"Alana, nothing released in this millennium is considered an 'oldie.' I will not tolerate that sort of talk in this household, young lady."—that I let myself relax and enjoy the reprieve.

I wasn't lying when I told Charlie I wouldn't trade my family for anything, I decided as I grabbed another apple to peel. *They're the best.*

And that, of course, was the moment when my great-aunt Selma barged through the back door with her grandson Pete trailing behind her, seated herself at the kitchen table where Mom had laid out a bunch of pie crusts that needed crimping, and began grilling me like a wartime prisoner.

"What's the story with Junior Nutter, Hunter?" Selma

spread dough into pie plates with gnarled fingers and trimmed the edges with the ease of long practice. "You paid two thousand dollars so you could dress him up like a feathered Chippendale and bring him to the Stuffin'?"

My paring knife slipped against the apple in my hand, and I nearly nicked my palm. "I bought him to help me renovate the event barn. The costume was just..." I coughed. "Fun."

Selma snorted so hard, the bedazzled pilgrim hats on her sweatshirt danced. "You're telling me you bid on him to do renovations? *Psssht*. Nonsense. Boy doesn't look like he ever buckled on a tool belt. Now, if you were lookin' for a Nutter who can get the job done, you shoulda bid on a strapping kid like his cousin Skip. He worked a shift at the Thrifty Nickel with me one time, and that boy can *haul*. Hoo-ee, but I wish I had someone like that around."

Alana and I exchanged a glance, then looked at Pete, who'd wrestled on the state all-star team in high school and was now a roofer. He was currently sitting silently beside his grandmother, munching a sliver of raw pie crust his grandmother had trimmed off. "You've got Pete." I pointed my paring knife in his direction. "He's strong."

"Nah. Pete's a good boy, but he wouldn't know which end of a hammer to pick up if I didn't keep a close eye on him. Isn't that right, Pete?" She patted Pete's knee with firm affection, and Pete rolled his eyes. "Besides, if I'm hiring out a job, I want me a young man who's gonna give me some *eye candy*." She wiggled her gray eyebrows meaningfully.

Alana and I exchanged another look. Selma was eighty if she was a day, so *young* could mean a lot of things.

"Now, if you were looking for eye candy, Hunter," Selma went on matter-of-factly, "you made a decent choice 'cause those Nutter boys are as cute as they come. Real flexible too. That's why they always make such a good showing at the apple bobbin' festival every fall. I always say Johnsons are best for Lickin', but nobody bobs like a Nutter."

The mental image this produced made me squeeze my apple so tightly that the damn thing shot out of my hand and rolled across the kitchen floor.

"Uh. Oops." My cheeks went hot, and I refused to meet Alana's eyes. "Slippery little things. Let me just…" I grabbed my fallen apple and brought it to the sink to rinse it.

"That's *such* an interesting observation, Aunt Selma," Alana said with overblown innocence. "I wonder what Jacksons are best at."

Selma's brow lowered, and her eyes narrowed. "You puttin' me on, girly? On this, the day of our family's triumph?" Her small shoulders straightened, and she spoke with terrible dignity. "Jacksons are made and meant for the *Stuffin'*, and don't you forget it."

This time, the apple *and* my knife both hit the inside of the sink with a clatter that had my mom looking up in concern from the cookies she was frosting.

"Maybe you better put down the sharp objects, baby," she said. "In fact, why don't you sit down and tell us all about—"

"I'm fine," I insisted. "*Fine.*" I focused my gaze on the bowl of sliced apples I'd been assembling. "But could we please talk about something that's not the Bobbin' or the Lickin' or the… the *Stuffin'*?"

"I had no idea festivals made Hunter so tetchy," Pete whispered to his grandmother loud enough for the whole kitchen to hear.

I changed my mind about my family being the best and briefly considered putting myself up for adoption.

"Back to your earlier point, Aunt Selma," Alana cut in.

"I don't know if all Nutters are handsome, but some of 'em are strange as a three-dollar bill."

"Thank you." I nodded. "*Yes.*"

"I don't mean Jun—Charlton," she continued with an eye roll. "I was thinking of Elmer Nutter, the mechanic over in Dooberville. He bases the price of an oil change on what the 'moon goddess is calling him' to charge, so you never know how much it'll be until you get there. I wanna know if the moon goddess is thinking to run a Black Friday sale."

"Elmer's probably just looking to make a quick buck, no moon goddess about it. He's the kind of guy who'd steal his grandmother's own pie crust right as she was getting ready to fill it." I lifted an eyebrow at Pete, who was shoving dough into his gullet with abandon, and he froze. "Pretty rude, wouldn't you agree?"

Pete grunted and tossed the last piece of dough he'd stolen back onto the table. I nodded in satisfaction. There were plenty of pie crusts, all stacked up between pieces of waxed paper, because my mom had gone with (gasp!) store-bought dough this year, but it was the principle of the thing.

Tetchy, my ass.

Pete got up and went to the fridge to grab a beer, gifting us all with the sight of a little too much butt crack. When he turned back around, he said, "Elmer's alright. Can't kiss worth shit, but his other oral skills make up for it."

He cracked open a can of beer and meandered out of the kitchen toward the ball game playing in the family room like he hadn't just dropped a bomb.

The rest of us stared after him in shock.

"Did he...?" I began faintly.

"My stars," Great-Aunt Selma whispered. "My Pete's been moved by the power of the Stuffin'. Ain't that somethin'?"

"Oh, for the love of— If Pete's gay, it's got nothing to do with the Stuffin'," I grumbled.

"I don't know," Alana said, a thread of laughter in her voice. "I'm no expert, but I think it might have something to do with that."

I shot her a dirty look.

My mom clasped a hand to her décolletage. "Well, I think it's great. I wonder if Cindy Ann's put him on her list of eligible LGBTQ bachelors."

"Probably." Alana reached over and grabbed the dough sliver Pete discarded and dropped it in her own mouth. "Please tell me y'all know Pete's hooking up with Mr. Pascal from the library. It's been going on for like... *weeks*."

Great-Aunt Selma and I gave Alana identical shocked-church-lady stares, which was lowering.

"It *has*?" Selma demanded.

Alana smirked. "Yep. Pretty sure Pete's bi, not gay. He was still seeing Mayu Yamada there for a while. I'm low-key suspicious he was dating them both together at one point, although I don't think Mr. Pascal's into women."

Selma gasped. "Cheating? My grandson? Now, *that* I do not hold with. Pete will be hearing about this on the way home, you'd best believe."

"Actually, open relationships are—" Alana began, but I slashed a finger across my throat before she could serve up an impromptu lesson in polyamory.

"Not a thing we'll be talking about today," I finished. I gave Selma a smile. "Especially since it's *Stuffin'* day, right? But your holiday centerpiece, on the other hand... How's that coming along?"

Great-Aunt Selma's face lit up in excitement as she described the various gourds and dried corn stalks she'd sourced for her decor.

The knowing grin my mother shot me had a tinge of pride in it that made me feel smug... for about twenty minutes, until Selma remembered there was something much more interesting to talk about than cornucopias.

"But enough about my mums and Pete's revelations. What happened with the turkey-Nutter, Hunter? And how'd Amos finally get him back to town, anyway? Roberta overheard Cindy Ann saying Junior has some kind of bigshot job up in Chicago. I figured that's why he never came around anymore."

"I guess so. Fancy office job in logistics and distribution," I said. "Distribution means..." I realized I was quoting Charlie and forced myself to stop. "Er. Anyway. Sounds boring, but he seems to like it."

My mom made a disapproving noise. "Just because *you* can't think of anything worse than being stuck inside all day doesn't mean it isn't a good job for the man. I'm sure he loves it as much as you love your plants."

I thought back to his reaction when he'd defended his job. "I don't think he loves it," I said slowly. "Not all of it, anyway. He might be proud of it, but that's not the same thing. Anyway." I shrugged. "None of my business."

"Hunter Jackson." My mother put down her pastry whisk and faced me with a glare. "Now, you know I'm not one to involve myself in my children's lives—"

"You're not? I mean... no! No, you're definitely not," I agreed swiftly when she set her hands on her hips. "Never in a million years."

She nodded, accepting this. "But you and Junior Nutter have always been friends, so you just stow that attitude right this minute. I bet Junior's job is stable, and stability's important when you're living in a big city."

"Or even if you're not," Selma interjected. "Life wasn't

all that easy for Junior and Katie-Bird after his daddy left. If the Nutters didn't own half the land around here and Amos hadn't made sure the two of them had a place to live, well..." She shook her head.

I frowned. Charlie and I had never talked about that stuff back when we were kids. My own parents had experienced rough years here and there, when a crop didn't perform well or market prices went down, but I'd never worried much about having everything I needed or even about finding odd jobs to afford the things I wanted. Looking at it as an adult, though, it was easy to see how a kid like Charlie might not have seen the Thicket as a land of opportunity... and why he might be so proud of his big Chicago job today.

But still.

"We're not friends, Mom," I corrected, focused on removing an apple peel in one long strip. "Haven't been for years. And he's not Junior anymore. He's Charlie."

It wasn't until I'd finished peeling my apple and looked up that I noticed the whole room had gone quiet and all three women were staring at me.

"What?" I demanded.

"My stars," Selma whispered again. "You got it bad for the Nutter."

"No! What? *No.* Didn't you hear me say we weren't friends? Because we're not." My face joined the oven on its preheat cycle, and I imagined it was as red as the apple skins I was peeling.

"Oh, Hunter." My mother's smile was a soft and melty thing. "Isn't that wonderful? After all these years, you and Junior—"

"*Charlie*, and no." I drew a circle in the air around her face. "Whatever you're thinking here, you're wrong.

Remember how he doesn't live here anymore? Remember how he left? Remember how he... he *stole*..."

I couldn't finish this statement, even to make a point. I wasn't sure I believed it myself anymore.

"Stole, did you say?" Aunt Selma pursed her lips. "Well, now, if the boy's a criminal, that's a different story. We should probably let the sheriff know. Wouldn't be the first time a Nutter broke the law around here. Remember when Eulalia Nutter got caught in the ten-items-or-less line with no fewer than *thirteen* items on the belt?"

My mother swatted my ass with the back of a wooden spoon. "Stop spreading rumors." To Selma, she added, "Ignore him. He's talking about the turkeynapping from way back when."

"Oh, *that*." Selma sat back in her seat and waved a hand as though this was no big deal.

"Hey, now. It was pretty important to me," I said, all offended dignity. "At the time."

"Boy, you must be the only turkey in town who didn't realize he took your bird 'cause he was sweet on you," Selma explained. "Charlton wanted to get your attention."

To my shock, my mother nodded.

"M-my attention?" I sputtered. "How the heck did you figure that? You don't hurt and betray someone you're *sweet on*. And *you* said maybe he'd got above his raisin' like his daddy," I accused my mother. "You said that."

"Baby, you were so upset about Dolly Parton I'd have told you aliens abducted the boy if I thought it would lift your spirits." My mom rolled her eyes. "Figures the one time in your entire life you listened to me was *that* moment."

My dad wandered into the kitchen and pecked a kiss on

Mom's cheek before stealing one of my apple slices. "Tell me he's not talking about that turkey."

My mom made a face, and my dad sighed. "Bud." He clapped a hand on my shoulder. "Get over it, I beg you. Dolly was missing half a day, and he went on to live a fine life until just a few years ago."

"A spoiled rotten life," my mom said fondly. "If I didn't give him dinner scraps, he'd chase me back into the house."

We took an unspoken moment of silence for the memory of Dolly Parton.

"He was a good bird," I said on a sigh.

Dad took me by the shoulders and turned me to face him. "Son, tough talk incoming. How'd you like it if I still brought up the time you lost your drawers in Bull Lake and clung to the dock until I came in and retrieved them for you?"

My preheating oven face was ready to broil. "That bathing suit was too big." I stuck my chin in the air. "And I'd have gotten them myself if I'd been able to swim then."

"Uh-huh. But would you like it if I brought up something that happened when you were, what? Ten?"

"Charlie was fourteen when he took Dolly."

"And my point stands," Dad said. "Figure out why this incident is still stuck in your craw, and move on." He squeezed my shoulders before letting go to clap his hands. "Now, I'm going to need to test someone's dessert before tomorrow on the off chance you're trying to poison the rest of us. Who has a sample for me?"

As everyone fought off his attempts to sneak a sweet treat, I thought about my dad's words.

Why *had* it stuck in my craw?

I remembered the moment when I'd realized Dolly was

missing. Remembered wishing Junior was there because he was the most understanding person I knew. When he *had* come by, carrying Dolly gently in a pillowcase, I hadn't understood at first... and then I had. I'd shouted at him, demanded an explanation, but he'd just stood there looking guilty, his mouth opening and closing like he'd forgotten how to speak, dragging his toe over the dirt out by the barn. He'd run away from my house, and later the town, without ever giving me the explanation I'd wanted. That I'd *deserved*.

And maybe that explained why I'd been mad back then, but it didn't explain why I'd reacted with anger when Charlie came back. I was old enough now to know that no one should be held responsible for the stupid stuff they did as a fourteen-year-old. And hearing that he might have done it because he was "sweet on me" made it particularly hard to stay angry... or to think about all of the reasons Charlie and I shouldn't finish what we'd started in the barn.

When we finally got the last of the desserts out of the oven and left them cooling on the counter, the sun had sunk below the tree line on the far side of the property. I stretched out my aching shoulders and smoothed a hand over my beard. "I'm about ready to head home," I said to no one in particular. "Long day, bad sleep. I feel rode hard and put away wet."

"Too much Dickel will do that," Alana singsonged, and I gave her a disgruntled look.

"You *should* go home, sweetie," my mom agreed. "You can't go to the Johnsons' Prep Party looking like that."

"Shi—*shoot*. I forgot Prep Party."

Cindy Ann Johnson's so-called Black Friday Prep Party had been conceived as a chance for all the bargain hunters of the Thicket to pore over Cindy Ann's super-secret early copies of the Black Friday sales circulars that would appear in the following day's newspaper. In theory, savvy shoppers would spend time mapping out a battle plan for Friday's shopping, with a goal of knocking out their Christmas gift purchases in one fell swoop.

In reality, the party was mostly a gossip session—as though the Thicket didn't have enough of those—and a chance for anyone football-minded to make predictions about the big Thanksgiving games, while Black Friday shopping continued to be a chaotic hot mess with zero strategy.

"Count me out," I said, leaning in to kiss my mom's cheek. "I'm whipped."

Mom pinned me with a glare. "Did I mention it's a command performance? I insist on having *both* of my children there."

Great-Aunt Selma chimed in. "It's a tradition."

"Yeah, bro," Alana parroted. "Tradition."

The problem with this particular tradition was that Cindy Ann Johnson was besties with Katie-Bird Nutter—back when they'd lived in the Thicket, Katie-Bird, Cindy Ann, and my mom had been inseparable—which meant Charlie would likely be at the Prep Party. And if he was there, I'd be right back into blue-ball territory, only this time, I'd be painfully, awkwardly hard while in front of my entire family.

"Sorry, I'm bucking tradition," I called as I headed down the porch steps. "See y'all tomorrow."

But if I thought avoiding the party would mean avoiding Charlie, I was dead wrong.

Chapter Seven

Charlton

I LEFT the Jackson place with blue balls I hadn't experienced in a very, very long time.

As I adjusted my hips in the hard seat of my uncle's side-by-side, I muttered a curse under my breath. It wasn't the first time Hunter Jackson had caused such a physical reaction in me.

Fortunately, the cold air on the drive back over the hill to my uncle's farmhouse worked wonders for clearing my head and calming me down. Though my muscles ached pleasantly after the time spent sanding the floor, I knew the physical labor would help me sleep tonight...

Because sleeping was exactly what I'd be doing.

I'd told Hunter the—whatever it was—between us wasn't over, but that was my dick talking. The idea of me turning up at his place later to resume our hookup was pure foolishness.

For one thing, I wasn't sure how I felt about the man. Oh, sure, he was every bit as handsome and compelling as he'd ever been, and the very sight of him triggered a response in me that felt like it had been hardwired back in middle school. And when we got to talking—in the moments when Hunter forgot he was angry, at least—I could see glimpses of the boy I'd once liked better than anyone. That easygoing boy who'd loved his family and his town with a steadfast devotion had grown into an ambitious, successful man, but he still had an inner core of kindness that made him respect a person's chosen name and worry their legs might be chilly, even when he was angry enough to parade them around in a turkey costume to settle a grudge. He was the sort of person anyone would be proud to have in their life.

But maybe because we'd known each other long ago, that man knew exactly how to get under my skin. In the moments he remembered he was angry—about Dolly Parton, no less—he had an uncanny way of poking at spots I hadn't known were tender. He riled me up more than anyone ever had... and, I admitted to myself, made me think about things I'd been carefully ignoring for a long while, like how satisfied I really was with my life in Chicago. Which wasn't particularly helpful since I'd be going back to that life in three short days.

It would probably be best for both of us if I kept my distance until then.

As soon as I pulled up to the farmhouse, my little cousin Jack came racing out the front door and down the porch steps. "Finally! What took you so long, Junior? We're late to the Johnsons'!"

"The Johnsons'?"

Jack looked at me like I was a brick short of a full load. "Sure. The Black Friday Prep Party, where folks pretend to care about shopping sales." He rolled his eyes broadly. "But there's *barbecue*. Red Johnson gets his smoker out, and he cooks up, like, a whole pallet of ribs, and Parrish—have you met Parrish? He runs, like, all of the Partridge Pit Barbecue restaurants—he brings all these special sauces, and his husband, Diesel—that is to say, Parrish's husband, not Red's, on account of Red's married to Cindy Ann—sometimes brings Wattle along, and he's a heavy son of a gun—Wattle, not Diesel... although, really, *both*—and he plays hide-and-seek with the kids."

I stared at Jack, my head whirling as I tried to make sense of all these names. "Wattle plays hide-and-seek?"

"Of course not. Wattle's an obese, flightless turkey." Jack gave me a pitying look. "Turkeys can't play hide-and-seek, Junior, don't you know that? Anyway." He bounced on the balls of his feet. "Ribs?"

My stomach growled loud enough for both of us to hear it, and I laughed. "Yes. Just let me get cleaned up."

I hurried through a shower and pulled on clean jeans and a sweater before double-timing it back down the stairs.

My mother lifted an eyebrow at me. "Hungry?"

I smiled. "You know it. And I have fond memories of Red's barbecue."

She laughed and looped her arm through mine as we made our way out of the house to join the throng of family members hopping in various vehicles. "You had a busy day. You must've worked up an appetite." She shot me a side-ways look. "People at the Stuffin' seemed tickled by your costume."

"Yeah." I grinned, remembering. "Everyone was very sweet. You know, I think people around here are nicer than I gave them credit for." I shrugged. "It's different, seeing them through adult eyes."

"It's true. The Thicket is a special place, and I'm glad you're realizing that. But..." She pulled me to a stop near Amos's truck. "Are you sure *everyone* was sweet to you?"

I frowned. "I mean... I think so? Everyone who talked to me had something nice to say."

My mom huffed. "I meant Hunter Jackson, Charlton."

"Oh." I rubbed the back of my neck. "Him."

"Yes, him. Don't suppose you'd like to tell me why my child was walking around dressed like a turkey?"

"Well, you and I had that niceness bet," I ventured. "I was being nice. He did buy me at the Biddin' after all."

She gave me a distinctly unimpressed look.

"Hunter may have had some... unresolved feelings about the Great Turkey Incident," I admitted.

"Because you never told him what actually happened," Mom surmised. "Did you?"

"Hardly matters anymore," I said, trying to make myself believe it. "He lives here in the Thicket. I live in Chicago. The past is the past."

"If you say so," she murmured, pulling open the back door. "But sometimes the past isn't all that easy to let go of."

As we rode the short distance to the Johnsons', the warm sound of family banter washed over me, and it was easier to block Hunter out of my mind. It was funny how quickly I'd gotten used to their noise and shenanigans... and how much I'd started to enjoy it. This time, when my cousin Jory teased me about being the "biggest turkey to ever walk around the Thicket," I reminded him that, pound for pound, I was also the most expensive turkey.

"Y'all are just jealous," I told Jory smugly. "'Cause nobody'd pay five dollars to see those spindly drumsticks."

Then I laughed out loud when Jory howled in outrage, and Jordan thumped me appreciatively on the back.

Amos met my eyes in the rearview mirror and winked, and I remembered what Hunter had said about family. *They're loud and interfering sometimes, and you might not enjoy every minute of their company, but they're* yours. Tonight, I felt the truth of that.

I settled back in my seat, watching as twilight washed over the Thicket. There was something familiar and almost restful about this place and these people. Like, I knew before we even arrived that Cindy Ann would fuss over me, tell me how grown up I was, and try to feed me until I was sick to my stomach. I knew Red would ask me about football and make sure I hadn't somehow become a Bears fan in the decade I'd been living in Chicago. And I knew my mother would take every opportunity to slip my recent promotion into the conversation as often as possible.

For as much as some things in the Thicket had changed while I was gone, the essential truths about life here hadn't and probably never would... and that was more comforting than I'd imagined.

"Who else is going to be there tonight?" I asked. "I thought I saw Brooks at the Biddin', but I wasn't sure. Is he home for the holidays?"

Jory turned around from the passenger seat with a comical look of disbelief on his face. "Brooks Johnson's been back in the Thicket for years and years. How'd you miss that?"

My mom bumped her shoulder against mine. "He and his husband, Mal, renovated an old farmhouse in town. Cindy Ann is over the moon to have all three of her kids here now."

"You said he was gay, but I didn't know he'd moved back here. Wow." I knew that, like me, Brooks had left the Thicket, and I'd imagined it was because he'd felt stifled here just as I had. Knowing he'd come back and built a life here was... well, strange. I wondered what had changed for him.

Once we arrived at the Johnsons', I was swarmed with a mix of old familiar faces and curious new ones. I hadn't had the chance to talk to much of anyone at the Biddin' the night before, but now that I was here, I enjoyed seeing people I remembered from before and meeting the new members of the town.

The place was packed with people, and the smoky scent of barbecue mingled with the tart, boozy aroma of "spiky sweet tea"—Cindy Ann's secret family sweet tea recipe, which her "adorable bonus son" Mal had "jazzed up a little" —and the overwhelming spice of the homemade potpourri on the table under the gallery of cow art in her entryway. The combination was a reminder of my childhood and brought long-forgotten memories flooding back.

"Dude, come with me. The cool kids are out back," Brooks said, grabbing my elbow and yanking me toward the sliding glass doors.

Outside, I found a bunch of camp chairs arranged around a fire pit, most of them occupied by people from our generation. There was enough of a nip in the air to keep my mom's generation safely inside with the children under their watchful eyes, while the teenagers had taken off to parts unknown, despite Cindy Ann's instruction that there'd be no "canoodling" at her house.

Brooks beamed at me as he paused behind the chair of a man with a mop of wavy brownish hair and bright blue eyes. "Junior, I want you to meet my husband, Mal. Mal, baby, this is Junior Nutter. We grew up together, until he took off for greener pastures... and then I did."

"Charlton," I corrected, shaking the man's hand. "Nice to meet you." Brooks's partner looked like the least likely person to have chosen life in Licking Thicket, which made me undeniably curious about their story. "So, you two met in New York, I take it? And... decided to move back to the Thicket for some reason?"

"Not quite." Mal laughed. "Believe it or not, we met right here. I was a beautiful, mysterious artist who'd come to town for the Lickin' Festival, and Brooks was the local golden boy on hiatus from his Big Job in the Big City. I defeated him in the Lickin' Lope." He pressed a hand to his chest and fluttered his eyelashes at his husband. "He lost the race but won my heart."

Brooks rolled his eyes and plopped down in the seat beside Mal's. "More like I handed you victory after your pail malfunctioned." He grabbed Mal's hand and kissed his palm. "And *then* I lost the race and won your heart."

Mal snorted, but I noticed he didn't let go of Brooks's hand either.

"You're omitting a few crucial details, boys." A woman across the fire flipped her blonde ponytail in such a familiar way that I remembered her immediately. "If it weren't for the folks of the Thicket, you two would probably still be dancing around each other all these years later."

"Ava? Ava Ivey?" I guessed.

She gave me a friendly smile and rested a protective hand on her very pregnant belly. "Ava Siegel now. And this is my husband, Paul." She gestured to the man beside her.

"Her long-suffering husband," Brooks teased. "Foot massages every night for eternity. Right, my little Paul?"

Paul made a noise of disagreement. "Nonsense. Whatever my darling bride needs, I'm happy to provide." He gazed at her adoringly.

"He wouldn't be massaging nearly as often if he could keep from knocking her up," Mal commented.

"Malachi!" Ava sat forward with narrowed eyes. "This baby was planned and every bit as wanted as the last three."

Mal grinned widely, and she *hmphed.* "Just for that, I'm giving Charlton the full, unabridged version of your twisted love story."

I sat down, and she proceeded to do just that—with "helpful" commentary from Brooks's brother, Dunn; Dunn's husband, Tucker, a large, tattooed man I recognized from the Stuffin' who appeared to be the Diesel-person Jack had mentioned; and Diesel's husband, Parrish—until Brooks turned the tables and began telling the tale of how Dunn had fallen for his doctor husband. By the time Cindy Ann's voice called that supper was ready, we were all in tears from laughing so hard.

As they talked, it became clear that these couples were an accepted, even *beloved*, part of a town that had grown and diversified even more than I'd realized in the past fifteen years, and for a split second, I almost wished I lived here so I could spend more time around the fire with them.

Almost.

Because while the town might be thriving, it still couldn't hold a candle to Chicago in terms of career opportunities, at least in the field of logistics. And I liked my "boring" logistics job. I enjoyed the challenge of creating and optimizing distribution and logistics strategies. Granted, it wasn't as fun doing it for a large corporation mired in regulations and red tape, but using my brain to increase company profits was rewarding. What could I possibly find to do around here that would—

"Charlton, honey?" Cindy Ann called, jolting me back to the party. "Get a move on if you want ribs!"

I shook my head to scatter my ludicrous thoughts. Had I really been thinking of moving back to the Thicket? Seamus would die laughing.

I jogged back to the house, where the food tables were

set up, and took a swig of spiked sweet tea from a red Solo cup someone handed me. My eyes roamed around the grouping of people before I realized what had been niggling in the back of my mind since arriving.

"Where's Hunter?" I asked Brooks before thinking it through.

Brooks's eyebrows shot up, and a smirk teased the corner of his mouth. "Why you asking? You planning some turkey costume payback?"

"No! Jeez. I just know you're good friends because your moms are good friends, and he lives across the street, and..." I clamped my mouth closed to stop myself from talking, noticing for the first time how many people around us were not-so-stealthily listening in. "Never mind."

"Hunter stayed home, Charlton," Hunter's sister Alana called from the other side of the table, making sure that anyone who hadn't already been listening before couldn't help hearing now. "He said he was whipped. I took that to mean he was tired. From all the *sanding*."

Her eyes twinkled in the warm light, and I glanced away, my eyes bouncing over every person standing around the table and every item on it before looking back at Alana.

"Oh," I said. "Right. Good."

She bit her lip and hesitated before speaking. "You know, he seemed a little..." She waved a hand. "Off."

"Off?" I repeated. "Off, like upset?" I couldn't stand the idea he might be angry about what had happened between us earlier.

"Tetchy," her cousin Pete interjected around a mouthful of bread roll from further down the buffet. "*Extra* tetchy."

Alana shot him a look. "I would have said... well, he admitted he hadn't slept well last night, and he wasn't feeling so good this morning, so I worry he might be..." She bit her lip again, and her eyes went sad.

I thought I heard Brooks snicker next to me, but I was too focused on Alana to wonder what he was laughing about.

"Sick?" I supplied. "You think Hunter might be sick?"

She sighed. "Yes. I really do. But you know how stubborn Hunter can be, and he wouldn't thank me for making a big deal of it." She waved her hand in the air again and summoned a brave smile. "Never mind. I'm sure he's fine. I'll check on him tomorrow if he doesn't show up for dinner. Boy, these ribs look amazing."

My gaze bounced around the table again, this time accusingly, but no one met my eyes. Hunter was ill while his so-called "friends" and family members had been standing around having fun? Not a single one of them had missed the party to stay with him?

I didn't care how stubborn Hunter was, the poor man lived by himself in a house he'd built near his greenhouses on his family property—my cousins had supplied me with that tidbit of knowledge the night before—and it didn't seem right that he was all alone.

My back teeth squeezed painfully together, but I forced myself not to volunteer. Hunter's welfare wasn't my business. Lurleen had always doted on Hunter, and Alana adored him. If they knew he'd stayed home from an event he normally would have attended, they'd look in on him before tomorrow. Surely. And, in any case, I was the last person he'd want to show up when he wasn't feeling himself.

But even after Alana began chatting to Quinn about the event barn project and everyone had moved outside with their food, I couldn't let go of my worry.

Three hours later, I couldn't stand it anymore. I threw the blankets on my bunk bed back and snuck out of bed, tugging on my clothes and tiptoeing out of the house.

When I got to the side-by-side, I silently thanked Uncle Amos for trusting his neighbors enough to leave the keys in the vehicle. At least when I embarked on my ridiculous midnight run to check on Hunter Jackson, I did it stealthily.

Chapter Eight

Hunter

I couldn't stop thinking about the damned turkey—and for once, I didn't mean Dolly Parton.

After all the revelations of the day, I was seeing Charlie in a whole new light. He was a good sport. A kind person. The sexiest man ever to wear a bird costume. And now that the last of my anger had left the building, it was really hard to remember why I shouldn't just enjoy as much time with him as I could, in every sweaty, fulfilling way I could.

And that was why there was *no* way I could show myself at the Johnsons' house tonight. The last time I'd seen Charlie, I'd begged to suck his cock, and we both knew it. I wasn't all that great at hiding my emotions at the best of times, and if I felt Charlie's molten-hot gaze on me at any point or caught even the slightest glimpse of wanting in his eyes... well, the Great Turkey Incident would be nothing compared to the scandal that followed.

I stretched my neck from side to side for the millionth time as I looked around my small house. I hadn't been lying when I said I was tired, but for some reason, I couldn't sit still. Even though there was a new episode of *Virgin River* waiting for me on Netflix, I found my mind wandering too fast and far to concentrate on it. My thoughts felt like a Formula One race populated by errant, hyperactive toddlers.

Out of desperation, I turned to the kitchen to busy myself with unnecessary chores. Everyone's fridge needed cleaning out from time to time, right? It was better than stomping across the street and making a public spectacle of myself.

I shuddered at the thought.

I emptied the food out of my fridge until the sink was full of dirty leftover containers and various sauce bottles and bags of veggies covered the countertop of my small kitchen island. Once everything was out of the fridge, I sprayed the interior down with cleaning solution and began to scrub.

It was ridiculous to be this obsessed with someone I hadn't even spared a thought for in over a decade, anyway, I reasoned. It was great that I wasn't angry anymore, but Charlie and I still weren't friends, and we weren't likely to be. He was a nice guy, but I knew plenty of nice guys. Had been attracted to lots of 'em too. Nothing about Charlie was special...

So why did the knowledge that he'd be leaving town in a few days make me feel nearly as devastated as I'd been the first time he'd left? And why was it suddenly so clear that my anger all these years hadn't been about the dang turkey at all but about the fact that my friend had left me and hadn't seemed to care?

That didn't change anything, of course. Even if I loved Charlie—and I didn't, because you couldn't fall that hard for anyone in a matter of hours, no matter how sweet and funny and kind he was—the distance was a deal breaker. I wouldn't be able to make a life in the city. I needed to be outside with my feet on the ground and my hands in the soil. I needed to feel the warm pressure of sunshine on my back and the damp curl of morning mist against my skin.

I scrubbed harder. *Why am I even thinking about this?*

I forced myself to make a list of the plant diseases I needed to read up on when I was forced inside during the next bit of bad weather. Maybe there was new research on how to battle the usual suspects.

Black spot.

Rust.

Botrytis blight.

Powdery mildew.

Bacterial canker.

I'd finished the list of diseases and was on to the most common pests when a firm knock startled me so badly I jumped, bumping my head on the fridge shelf.

Fuck.

The knocking came again, faster this time.

"Jesus, Alana," I muttered, rubbing my head as I crossed the room and reached for the door. "Figures the one damn time you actually knock instead of walking right in, you—Oh." I swallowed hard as the door opened to reveal a frowning face that did *not* belong to my sister. "Charlie. H-hey."

Suave, Hunter.

Charlie's eyes roved over my pained face, then down to my rumpled shirt, damp with sweat and cleaning products. I shifted on my bare feet, hating that I was such a hot mess when Charlie looked like sex in a sweater and smelled like vanilla cologne, fire pit, and... barbecue sauce?

In my defense, I'd convinced myself that he'd been kidding when he'd said he'd come over tonight. That he'd rethink things and realize that he didn't actually want me the way I wanted him—

"Oh, boy. Get inside and lie down right now," Charlie commanded. "Bed or sofa, up to you."

"Uh." I stared at him blankly, trying to recalibrate my thoughts. I couldn't deny that my dick was already on board just at the sound of his voice, but this seemed sudden. "Maybe... Let's have a drink first?"

Charlie nodded as he pushed inside. "Good idea. Hydration is important. I'll get it. Have you taken anything?"

"Taken... I... no?" I rubbed my head some more and watched in confusion as he kicked off his shoes. Charlie Nutter was in my space. *In my home.* God, I liked that way too much.

He tilted his head and looked at me. "What do you want, Hunter?"

I opened and closed my mouth like a guppy. Was he asking...? "I... whatever you... I mean... *huh?*"

Charlie's whole face twisted in sympathy. "You really must be sick."

"I'm not sick," I argued. But I frowned. He seemed so sure of himself it made me second-guess my own body. "I don't think?"

"Stubborn," Charlie sighed. He pushed the door closed, clasped my arm, and led me to the sofa, where he crouched on the floor between my knees and stared up at me. "How are you feeling?"

"Good," I managed. *Very* good when he shifted up and pressed himself against my knee. "I bumped my head a minute ago."

"*Tsk.*" One cool hand touched my forehead as if checking

for a fever, then pulled my own hand away from my bruised head so he could run gentle fingers over my scalp. "Are you light-headed? Do you think it might be a concussion?"

I *hadn't* thought so. Now, I wasn't so sure.

I grabbed his hand firmly in mine. "What's happening right now? Why are you here?"

Charlie sank back onto his heels, but I couldn't help but notice that his free hand rested on my thigh. His touch seared through the wash-worn flannel of my pajama pants and heated up my skin until it prickled.

"Alana told me you weren't feeling well. I came to see if you needed help."

I blinked at him. "I'm feeling fine. Why would she have...?" I closed my eyes with a groan. That meddling fucker.

"Sure you're fine." Charlie rolled his eyes. "Just like you were fine back in middle school baseball when you broke your wrist in the first inning and insisted on playing the rest of the game? You're in so much pain you're groaning, babe. Now, lie back and let me get you that drink and maybe a cold cloth for your head."

Suddenly, I was hit by the giggles like a preteen. My giddy excitement over his unexpected visit, the typical nosy meddling by my sister, the utter rush of his proximity, his unexpected (and incredibly arousing) use of the word *babe*, and the absolute ridiculousness of this latest misunder-standing was too much after all the shit that had already happened in the last twenty-four hours. I laughed so hard it was hard to catch my breath.

Charlie stared at me. He seemed this close to calling emergency services to request immediate transport to the nearest hospital specializing in traumatic brain injuries.

"I bumped my head in the fridge," I said, wiping my damp eyes. "It's no big deal. Really."

The concern in his expression didn't fade. Instead, he reached out and took my head in his hands, palpating gently with his fingers again as if searching for a goose egg or, worse, a crater.

The massage felt good enough to make me contemplate faking an actual injury, but I wasn't a good enough liar.

"I'm fine," I said softly. "I promise. Alana lied to you, probably because she's attempting to matchmake." I stifled a groan and added breathlessly, "But feel free to keep doing that."

Charlie's eyes met mine, and the tension between us rocketed deep into my gut. Time seemed to trip up, like balding tires trying to find purchase in sticky mud. His eyes dipped to my mouth before moving slowly back up to meet mine. Pulling in oxygen got harder, and I lost control over the surface of my skin. The blood flow in my body sounded like the low, loud buzz of airplane engines, which was weird since so much of it seemed to be shooting south to my groin.

I licked the taste of his gaze from my lips as I imagined what it would feel like to lean forward and take his mouth in mine. Late-day whiskers shadowed his face, and I could almost hear the catch of his prickles in my beard.

His fingers moved down until his thumbs brushed my cheeks. He seemed to realize what he was doing because he yanked his hands away like they'd been burned. It made sense since I was sure my cheeks had returned to the default lava state they tended to enjoy when this particular man was around.

"Glad you're okay," he grumbled in a strangely rough voice. "I should, ah... probably..." He looked around as if confused about where he was before slowly standing up and turning toward the door. My heart thundered in panic.

"It wasn't just about Dolly Parton!" I blurted, desperate to keep him here.

He turned back to face me, curious now.

"I mean... I mean, that's not the whole reason I was upset at you," I mumbled, mortified.

To my surprise, Charlie's expression morphed into a little smirk, and his dark eyes danced. "You mean to tell me you *haven't* been holding a grudge against me for fifteen years over a turkey? Because there's a costume around here that suggests otherwise..."

"Sarcasm isn't sexy, asshole," I lied. "And I said Dolly's not the *whole* reason. He's definitely *part* of the reason. That turkey was a beloved companion for twelve whole years after that incident. Followed me around as I built my business from scratch and never once left me with no..." I stopped speaking before I could finish my thought.

Dolly had never up and left me with no explanation. Unlike other people.

Charlie sighed and took a seat next to me on the sofa. "I'm glad he was a good companion. But... Hunter, I didn't hurt Dolly Parton. I would never have done hurt him. Or you."

I nodded slowly. I believed him. "So why did you take him?" I asked for the first time.

Charlie lifted his hand and hesitated before bringing it over mine and pulling my hand between both of his. It almost felt like he was grabbing hold of me to keep me from leaving until he'd had a chance to make his case. Regardless, the dry warmth of his fingers tangled in mine released some of the tension in my shoulders.

"Look, I... I'm not saying I handled things well," he

admitted. "I was doing the best I could, but looking back, there were better ways..."

I squeezed his hand. "And you were fourteen, so you didn't know them. Just tell me, Charlie."

"Right. Well. I came over to your place the morning of the competition to see if you needed any help transporting Dolly to the show, but your grandpa said you were busy upstairs getting your shirt and tie on. You'd been telling all of us at school about how you'd bathed him a couple days before and gotten him all shined up—"

"Only his beak," I corrected loftily. "According to the poultry competition handbook, entrants are only allowed to apply Vaseline to the bird's beak and toes. Otherwise, it might affect their proper tail carriage."

Charlie winced. "*Wellll*, yes. About that." He coughed lightly. "I, ah, wanted to see how nice Dolly looked, so I went out to his habitat while I waited for you, and... *thebirdwaslubed.*"

"The..." I shook my head. "Say again?"

"Dolly Parton. He was coated in lube," Charlie managed. "I mean, wattle to tail feathers, all the way down to his skin, just fucking *glistening* and slimy with it. So gunky that a bunch of straw and little rocks from his habitat were stuck to him like, um, little rhinestones?"

"That's not possible." I frowned. "How could..."

"Your sister was sitting off to the side, next to a few of your grooming tools, with the half-empty tub of Vaseline. She'd only smeared it up to her elbows by the time I found her. And she said, 'Charlie, look! Dolly and me are all pretty for the show! Hunter's gonna be so happy!'"

I groaned. Alana had been seven or eight at the time— young enough that I hadn't wanted her "help" getting Dolly ready for the show, old enough to be put out about that fact.

Many, many times, I'd had to rescue Dolly from her attempts to add glitter and ribbon to the bird's "wardrobe," and no matter how often I'd told her off or how many big-eyed looks she'd given me, she'd been persistent.

"I... I panicked," Charlie admitted. "I wiped Alana off and told her to go get changed, but that turkey would *not* wipe down. And I could just picture you coming out and finding Dolly like that, knowing Alana had done it. You'd have been so angry, and she'd have been heartbroken. She wanted to see Dolly get first prize as much as you did."

"So you took him."

Charlie nodded. "I only took him so I could bathe him. I meant to bring him back before you found out what happened. But when I got him to Uncle Amos's place..." He grimaced. "Have *you* ever tried to get five pounds of lube off a very pissed-off tom?"

I tucked my tongue into my cheek, suddenly fighting the urge to laugh. "Can't say I have."

"Zero out of ten, do not recommend, let me just tell you. Not to speak ill of the dead or whatever, but that bird was *fierce* when he didn't get his way. Nearly as stubborn as his owner. Look." He removed his hand from mine and pointed to a small silver crescent on the skin near his hairline. "Battle scar."

I reached up to run my fingertip over it. "I'm sorry," I said. "I didn't know."

He was so close. The warmth from his body and the scent of him were doing things to my stomach. Compelling as the story was, part of me—*most* of me—no longer cared about the past.

I wanted Charlie Nutter naked in the *present*. I wanted to run my hands along every inch of him.

"Then what?" I croaked, mostly because stripping him

down in the middle of a conversation that had been fifteen years in the making seemed rude.

He pulled my hand away from his face and brought it to his mouth for a soft kiss to my knuckles before keeping hold of it. "Then... I spent ten hours and an economy-sized bottle of Dawn dishwashing soap trying to clean petroleum jelly off a competition turkey. I emerged victorious, eventually... but by that time, you'd already missed the opportunity to take him to the competition." His mouth twisted. "So I brought him back to you."

"You never said a word, Charlie. Not about any of this—"

"I know. I... I thought about it. I planned to. And I knew you'd be disappointed, but I figured you'd understand I was just trying to help..."

I nodded. I definitely would have.

"But from the second you saw me with Dolly, you were so angry I could barely get a word in edgewise, and I... I didn't know how to tell you. Literally. My stomach flipped over like I was going to be sick all over your yard, and I couldn't make my mouth form the words, and poor Alana was there looking nearly as upset as you, and I... I just ran away. I told myself I'd wait a few days until you'd calmed down. But then I found out I was leaving. And I just figured... why ruin it? Why put this thing between you and your sister when I could take the blame and pretend it was all a silly prank? It seemed like..." Charlie took a deep, shuddering breath. "Like one last thing I could do for you since you'd been a good friend to me."

"I wouldn't have blamed Alana!" I said. "She was a little girl, for God's sake. She didn't know better."

Charlie's gaze met mine. "Maybe. I mean, yeah, I'm sure eventually you'd have been calm and rational about it.

But at fourteen? Anger and blame are par for the course at that age. I don't think calm or rational described either of us."

I frowned. I couldn't argue, given how long I'd spent blaming Charlie and being angry.

"And you know, Hunter," he went on, "you *know* that if folks in town knew what had happened, Alana wouldn't have lived it down. She'd have been the turkey-lube-girl all through high school. The girl who screwed up the turkey competition. Someone would probably bring it up at her funeral." One side of his lips twitched up, though there was no amusement in his eyes.

I squeezed my eyes shut as understanding dawned. "The way they do with you and your dad."

Charlie shrugged. "Kinda, yeah. And maybe *now* I can see that people aren't trying to be hurtful when they tease about that stuff and are even expressing support and love in a kind of ass-backward way, but... I certainly didn't know it then. And I didn't want that for Alana."

I hated how right he was.

"I've spent all this time blaming you," I said past a lump in my throat, "when you were just trying to help."

He reached out again and held the side of my head. The caress of his thumb across my cheek made my stomach tighten with need. "I cared about you," he said in a low voice. "I did then, and I do now. I didn't want you to hurt. I didn't want you to return to Dolly's pen and see your dream of winning the contest come to a swift end because of something that wasn't your fault."

"I made you dress up like a turkey," I choked out. "Jesus, Charlie. Why didn't you stop me?"

"I figured it'd be easier than sanding floors." His teeth flashed in a devastating grin. "And it wasn't so bad, really.

Everyone was really supportive, and a couple people grumbled about you taking this grudge too far. If anyone came off badly, it was you."

"No shit." I rolled my eyes. "I'm so fucking embarrassed." I wasn't sure if his hand began to pull me or if the movement was self-propelled, but I leaned in and buried my face in his neck to keep from facing him. "I'm so sorry," I breathed.

Charlie's fingers threaded through my hair, and his other arm wrapped around me, pulling me closer. After a few moments, his deep voice rumbled through us both.

"Make it up to me?"

Chapter Nine

Charlton

I COULD NO LONGER DENY WANTING him. Hunter was everything attractive to me in a man. Hardworking, muscular and fit, dedicated to his family, kind to his neighbors, and passionate. Hell, even his anger at me over a damned turkey turned me on.

My hands were drawn to him like magnets outside of my control, and when I realized he hadn't pulled away from my touch, I began to wonder if it was possible he'd let me do more than touch him. I wanted his lips on mine and his naked skin bared to me.

I wanted to get as deep inside of him, or him inside of me, as he'd let me. As soon as I'd suggested he could make it up to me, Hunter's eyes had widened, and his pupils had expanded.

"You..." He began hesitantly. "You want to..."

I let out a soft laugh before closing the distance between us and finally, finally getting my mouth on him again. The interrupted kiss in the barn earlier today seemed like it had been years ago, and I planned on making up for lost time now.

Hunter let out a guttural sound before surging forward and clasping the back of my head with his large hand, overwhelming me with the scrape of his beard against my face and the scent of…

"Have you been cleaning?" I said, pulling back with a grin. "You smell like bleach spray."

"Shut up," he said through a laugh. "Don't worry about it."

This time, he was the one who pounced. Hunter pushed me back onto the sofa and straddled me, returning to the kiss and to the firm hold he had on my head. I wrapped my arms around him and found the hem of his shirt before sliding my hands underneath it and up onto his bare back. The warmth of his skin was addictive, and my fingertips ached to memorize every plane. His tongue tasted faintly of oranges, and the nip of his teeth on my lips promised a partner who wasn't afraid to dominate.

Everything about Hunter fired me up. I wanted to both fuck him straightaway and take my time with him, slowing down to enjoy every moment of exploration.

I moved my hands down into the back of his pajama pants and felt the bare globes of his thick ass. A hungry groan escaped my throat. "God, I want you," I grumbled, squeezing his ass before teasing his crack with a finger. Just the idea of fucking him was making my dick throb. I couldn't imagine the orgasm I'd have from actually doing it. "Tell me you're up for it."

Hunter nodded and made an inarticulate sound of agreement. It was all I needed. I grabbed him under the ass and stood up from the sofa.

"Fuck, put me down! I'm too heavy," he cried.

"Have a little faith. I told you I could lift more than paperweights," I said with a wink, turning toward the door that presumably led to his bedroom. "Which way to your bed?"

He clung to me with his arms around my neck and his legs around my waist as I bumbled my way to his bedroom. When I saw the king-size bed in the center of the room, I dropped him on it and began stripping off my clothes.

"Get naked," I said, giving him a look that hopefully implied urgency. Because it was definitely an urgent situation.

Hunter scrambled to remove his pajamas and tee while I peeled off my jeans. My eyes stayed glued on him as he revealed glorious swaths of bare skin, muscled and still sun-browned from working outside.

"Fuck, you're a picture," I said, hearing the Tennessee slide into my voice the way it did in times of heightened emotion.

"And you," he said, nodding at me. "I take back everything I ever said about Peloton."

His teasing grin and bright eyes made my heart trip over itself. In another life, I could want more with him, much more, but in this life, I lived in Chicago and he lived in the Thicket. In this life, all we could have was this one night of hot sex... and I knew it would be hot because it already was. Even before touching him, Hunter made me feel like my orgasm was only a heartbeat away.

My eyes roved over him, landing on his hard cock standing proud from its nest of dark curls. He stroked it slowly while inspecting me the same way.

I stalked closer to him and crawled onto the bed before leaning over to kiss him again. As much as I wanted his dick and his ass, for some reason, kissing him was really doing it for me too.

His hands moved across my shoulders and back while

we kissed, and after straddling him, I pressed my hard cock against his. Both of us groaned through the kiss as our hips naturally found a rhythm that felt incredible.

I reached down to take us both in hand, reveling in the warm length of him sliding against me. "You feel so fucking good," I murmured against his lips before moving my mouth down to feast on his neck.

"Gonna come," he gasped. I immediately let go and pulled back, breaking contact to stop his orgasm. He made a choking sound of disappointment and whimpered. The sound went straight to my balls. "Want you. Fucker. Please."

I cupped his face and met his eyes. They were glassy with need, his face flushed and hair already a wreck from my fingers. This man was so fucking beautiful, and seeing him drunk with lust stole my breath. "Not yet."

I moved my mouth down his neck to his chest, nipping on the defined muscles there before pulling his nipples into my mouth one at a time to suck and pull. His legs came up and wrapped around my back as his fingers dug into my skull, and his hips lurched up, seeking relief.

"Patience," I urged, moving down even further until I could run my tongue through the dark hair on his abdomen and down to the dripping tip of his dick. I licked it before sucking the tip into my mouth and enjoying seeing the arch of his back and clench of his thighs.

"Fucking fuck," he gasped. He tightened his fingers in my hair. "Yes. Fuck. Just like that. More."

I wanted to tease him—ask if he wanted it just like that or if he wanted more—but I was too busy tasting him. The scent of him, warm and masculine in the crease of his thigh, made my dick even harder. I inhaled deeply before sucking him deeper.

Watching his reactions was almost enough to bring about my own release, but I didn't want that. I wanted to focus on his happiness, on his pleasure, sucking and swallowing around him until he finally grabbed the sides of my head and choked out my name.

Charlie.

Hunter had spent years calling me Junior the same way everyone else did. It had only taken him one correction to change it. He hadn't argued, hadn't tried to convince me I was wrong to want to be referred to by my real name. He'd simply respected my choice, even though it meant changing his own habits.

Despite holding the grudge about Dolly, he'd shown his respect for me in his compliance. I knew it wasn't easy. It had taken my own mother a long time to acquiesce, and it felt like there was absolutely no hope for most of my extended family. But Hunter had done it right away.

His body shuddered as I swallowed around him. My desire to fuck him was still there, and my dick was still hard, but I pulled off and moved to lie next to him, willing to wait for round two before seeking my own orgasm.

"Good?" I asked after his breathing began to steady. My voice sounded a little rough from the abuse.

"Fuck."

I snorted softly and reached over to brush damp tendrils of hair off his forehead. "Mmm. I'll take that as a compliment."

Hunter shot me a sheepish look. "Not sure it was your talent, to be honest. I was pretty teed up for it by the time you put your mouth on me."

I clapped a hand over my heart. "You wound me, sir."

His eyes danced. "Don't get me wrong. There's talent there, for sure. But I was... let's just say I might have discovered a disturbing kink of mine today." He lifted an eyebrow and shrugged. "Overgrown turkeys who moonlight as construction workers."

I laughed out loud. "Is that a common thing here in the Thicket?"

"Judging by the reactions at the Stuffin' today," he said darkly, "I'm definitely not the only one."

Laughing with a man in bed was something I hadn't done in a long time. Despite the years and distance, I felt more comfortable with Hunter than I had with many people in Chicago. Maybe it was because he'd known me long ago and understood my family history, or maybe because all the things about him that had called to me years ago were still there, only honed and amplified by time. Whatever the reason, I wanted to stay here and experience more of it....

But I knew that wasn't part of our unspoken agreement.

"I, ah... I should go," I said, breaking eye contact and looking around to remind myself where I might have put my clothes.

He reached out and grabbed my wrist. "Don't. Not... not yet." I glanced back at him over my shoulder. His face was serious for a split second before his expression morphed back into teasing. "At least stay until I can return the favor."

It was a flimsy excuse, but if that was what he was offering, I was damned well going to take it.

I leaned back in and stole another kiss, suddenly feeling like I had a limited allotment and needing to make every remaining moment of connection between us count.

We made out again like horny teens, kissing and feeling each other up until we were both rock-hard and gasping again. Our bodies were slick with sweat, saliva, and semen by the time I begged him to take me over the edge. My brain was a white static haze, and I couldn't even find the will to care *how* he made me come as long as he did… quickly.

"Hunter, *Hunter*. Fucking please. *Please*," I chanted as he toyed with me. His spit-slick fingertip teased my hole as his tongue tortured my cock. I tried to reach down to stroke myself, but he grabbed my wrist again and pinned it beside me on the bed.

"*No*."

I made an embarrassing noise that sounded too much like a whiny whimper for my comfort. His eyes met mine and locked on them as he finally breached my hole and found just the right spot as he upped the pace on my dick. I came screaming into my fist.

My stomach muscles clenched as my balls emptied into Hunter's mouth.

I felt spent. Empty. Hollow.

But I also felt vulnerable and fragile in a way that made me want to run.

I glanced over at Hunter as he moved up to flop next to me. His cheeks were flagged red, and his eyes were wet from gagging. Damp hair ringed his face, and his beard had a string of come in it.

"You're fucking stunning," I said without thinking. I thumbed away the string before I leaned over and kissed his swollen lips.

This kiss was different. Tired and slow, soft and sweet.

Utterly and completely terrifying.

"Now I really have to go," I said, forcing the words through my teeth and trying my hardest to accompany them with a smile.

Hunter's eyes widened in surprise for a moment before he did the same kind of forced smile. "Yeah. Yeah, obviously. Sure."

I moved off the bed to search for my clothes. The silence in the room crawled over my skin as I dressed. I couldn't stand it.

"You, ah, have big plans tomorrow with your family?" I asked.

This was a stupid question—anyone in the Thicket who didn't have big Thanksgiving plans with their own family would find themselves temporarily adopted by a family who had big Thanksgiving plans—but Hunter didn't call me on it.

"Yeah. Yep." He got up and slipped his own clothes back on. "Mom and Dad serve their meal around four. What about you?"

"I think we eat at noon. Uncle Amos deliberately does that so no one can watch the Packers play the Lions, and so we'll be done eating before the next game starts."

Hunter huffed out a laugh, and the sound released some of the tension in my shoulders. "Why the Packers hate?"

"I'm so glad you asked because I asked this very question last night, and now I can quote you chapter and verse. *Ahem*. Apparently, in 2012, the Tennessee Titans gave up fifty-five straight points to the Green Bay Packers before making one measly touchdown. To this very day, Amos still occasionally wakes up crying about it—a fact which Emmaline apparently knew before their marriage but which didn't stop her from marrying him anyway, which goes to show there's someone for everyone out there." Hunter laughed, and I grinned back. "Needless to say, there will be no Ackers-Pay on the television in the Nutter household. But Savannah says everyone watches it on their cell phones under the table, and Jaden said he'll distribute low-profile wireless earbuds to anyone interested."

This riveting football conversation lasted until we were

standing at the front door, the two of us shifting awkwardly as we tried to figure out how to say goodbye.

Hunter looked down at his bare feet, then at the door-knob, then at my chin before starting the circuit again. "You know, uh... if... if you want to watch the game highlights later..." He ran a hand through his hair before clutching the back of his neck, and his eyes flicked to mine again. "I have a subscription to NFL Sunday Ticket."

It was hard to describe how little I cared about the Packers game, and still, I found myself saying, "Yeah, maybe!"

At the same time, Hunter said, "Or not."

We both spoke again.

"Oops. I mean—"

"Sorry, you go ahead—"

I reached out and clapped a hand over Hunter's mouth before forcing him to meet my eyes. "I'd like to come over later tomorrow if I can. I'm not sure yet how things are going to go with the family, and I promised my mom I wouldn't bail on the important bits. But if you're still up for it when I'm done..." I moved my hand away and gave him my phone. "Put your number in?"

Hunter scraped his upper lip with his bottom teeth to hide a grin while he punched in the information. "Just text me," he said. "No big deal if not."

"Yeah, no, sure," I said intelligently. "Of course."

We stared at each other for another beat before I leaned over and pressed a kiss to the side of his mouth, staying there long enough to inhale him one last time. Even if I was able to come over, that would be hours and hours away, and I wasn't sure I could last that long without one more taste.

"Night," I said softly.

"Night," he breathed.

I made my way out of the warm house and into the cold dark. The freezing drive back to Amos's farmhouse was a blur, made grainy by memories and images of Hunter.

After taking a quick shower, I successfully snuck into the bunk room and fell into an exhausted sleep.

The next morning, I was awakened by various voices screaming from one end of the house to the other.

"You're missing the parade!"

"What channel's it on?"

"The internet, Uncle Amos! It's on the internet!"

I blinked my eyes open to see the sun streaming across the far side of the room. Everyone else was already up, and the room was a mess of discarded bedding, clothes, and shoes. After pulling fresh clothes on—nicer ones that would be appropriate for the celebration—I made my way downstairs in hopes of finding a vat of coffee.

My mom had taken up a spot next to one of the two large coffee makers. As soon as she saw me, she poured me a cup and gestured toward the kitchen table. "Savannah picked up some oat milk for you."

I blinked, absurdly touched, and turned to my cousin, who was sitting at the kitchen table with her feet propped on the chair beside her, demolishing a freshly baked cinnamon roll the size of her head. "Savannah, thank you. You didn't have to do that."

"Easy peasy," Savannah said around a gooey mouthful. She winked. "If we keep you happy, maybe you'll come back. I need a partner for trivia night down at the Tavern."

"Wait, wait, wait. No way are you bogarting Junior," Jory insisted, coming into the kitchen and plunking himself down at the table beside her. "Not cool, Savannah. We'll arm wrestle for him fair and square!"

My mother's eyes danced at me over the top of her own coffee mug.

I fell into a kitchen chair and doctored my coffee before worshipping it slowly and thoroughly. Family and friends moved in and out of the large kitchen, accompanied by waves of noise and the various scents of Thanksgiving dishes. From the direction of the dining room, I could hear the clink of silverware and china, along with the whispered gossip between two of my aunts as they set the table, and in the den, Amos was already instructing the little kids to be patient because Santa wouldn't show up until the end of the parade.

It was... nice.

Really nice.

Way nicer than I'd remembered.

For the past few years, I'd been so busy around the holidays that I hadn't even gotten to see my mother. I'd spent Thanksgiving in Chicago, tagging along with Seamus to sophisticated dinner parties that featured plenty of vegan options, six kinds of wine, and not a can-shaped cranberry sauce in sight. I'd told myself that was how sophisticated people celebrated Thanksgiving—no meddling family to placate, no chaos, no confusion—and I'd *liked* it... but never as much as the other guests seemed to.

Being here now was like spraying a mist of sentimental holiday comfort around me and letting the magic settle on my skin. I'd forgotten how good it could feel to be part of the rituals of a place. To have Aunt Charli demand that I taste-test her mashed potatoes while the kids yanked at my wrists and tried to pull me outside to play tag. To sit beside Emmaline at the overloaded table and have her gnarled fingers wrapped around mine while Amos said grace and encouraged every member of our huge family to state the one thing they were most thankful for this year. To have my mom, who was seated on my other side, knock her shoulder into mine companionably as she said, "I think I'm most thankful for... *niceness.* Aren't *you*, Charlton?" To have Amos's eyes find mine as he said, "I'm thankful *all* the family's home this year." And to swallow down the lump in my throat as I managed to croak out my own thanks a moment later.

After that, everyone fell on the food like they'd been starving since the previous November. Butter and gravy, conversation and laughter flowed around the room and out into the sun porch, where the smaller kids' table was set up. No one was foolish enough to disturb the happy mood by discussing politics or religion, and the only moment of controversy occurred when Jory, whose gaze had been directed at the phone in his lap for a good part of the meal, interrupted Amos's discussion of his heritage Guernseys by standing up from the table and screaming, "Wooo hooo! Hell, yeah! That's what I'm talkin' about!"

Without missing a beat, Amos had said, "Jory, son, I never knew you were so passionate about animal husbandry! From now on, I'm gonna make sure you help me with *all* the barn chores. No, no, don't need to thank me," Amos had added as a red-faced Jory attempted to stammer out a denial. "Your excitement is all the thanks I need." And then he'd sent me an amused wink that said he knew exactly what Jory had been excited about and he looked forward to Jory's attempts to weasel his way out of it.

This, *this*, was real Thanksgiving, this feeling of being known and accepted, of being loved and, even better, liked. It was *family*, exactly as Hunter said it was, and I knew a lot of people were able to find that feeling with people they weren't related to, but somehow, I never had.

I wasn't sure if I hadn't recognized the feeling when I was a kid, or maybe I'd been too hurt and angry about my dad to feel it at all back then—maybe I'd had to grow up and move away so that I could look back and see it for what it was—but when I'd whispered, "I'm thankful for belonging," earlier, I'd meant it down to my bones.

After dinner, everyone who hadn't been involved in cooking the meal worked on cleaning it up, packaging metric tons of leftovers into plastic containers, and washing nearly every dish in the house. Other folks went on "digestion walks" or took "digestion naps" or, in the case of my uncle Hess, poured themselves a stiff "digestive" whiskey with a splash of apple cider to be festive. Some people left to have dessert and spend time with their friends or another branch of their family, while new people arrived to take their places just in time for the football game to start.

Without intending to, I ended up sitting next to my cousin Buck, who was one of the new arrivals. For a solid hour, I listened to him tell an unbelievable tale that involved his "seed" being stolen by a notorious drug cartel, a daring rescue mission in Venezuela, a decoy "Horn," and how he and he alone had rounded up his enemies and saved the day in the end.

Very little of it had made sense until Amos had leaned over and murmured, "Horn of Glory is a video game Buck created, kiddo. You've never heard of it?"

As a matter of fact, I had—it had been all over the news a while back—I just hadn't had any idea that it had been created by a member of my own family or that the company was headquartered right here in the Thicket.

Suddenly, I remembered telling Hunter with total confidence that there were certain jobs—like art or running a tech company—that simply couldn't be done in the

Thicket. Now I understood his smug look, and I felt more than a little foolish. Both Mal with his art and Buck with his video game company seemed to be doing just fine living out their dreams right here, and I couldn't help wondering whether I was being shortsighted in thinking I couldn't do the same if I wanted to.

But... did I actually want to? Thanksgiving was one thing, but was living in the Thicket something I could actually see myself doing?

I was so deep in thought over this that when Amos nudged my shoulder and asked me to go with him to the far pasture to "deliver a holiday message to the good folks of the Thicket," I couldn't think up an excuse. So I rode shotgun and helped him swab each cow with a nontoxic livestock hair dye until they spelled out EVERYONE BELONGS IN THE THICKET...

And then collapsed into laughter a moment later when one of the cows, in Regina George–level *Mean Girls* move, head butted her way through the herd, pushing the others aside, collected a bunch of her friends, and went to stand on the far side of the field, leaving the remaining cranky cows to spell out OBSCENE, RIVETING HOLE.

Could I see myself living in the Thicket? I was starting to think I knew the answer.

When we returned to Amos's house, I started talking to Buck again, this time much more intentionally, and by the time I pulled myself away, it was nearly midnight.

My heart fluttered in my chest as I remembered my plans with Hunter, and I lost no time in sneaking out to the side-by-side for the drive to his place. But it wasn't until I was halfway there that I realized I'd never checked my texts to see if he even wanted me to come.

Chapter Ten

Hunter

After Charlie left my place the night before, I thought I'd spend so much time overthinking I'd never be able to get to sleep. Thankfully, though, I'd been so tired that I'd fallen asleep the minute my heart rate finally settled. I'd even managed to sleep in a little since I wasn't due at Mom and Dad's place until noon.

I got up and showered before throwing on a pair of work coveralls and packing my nicer clothes in a duffle bag. Hopefully, I'd have a couple of hours to catch up on some work at the greenhouses before my family inevitably called to ask me to come earlier.

As soon as I entered the warm, humid air, I felt my muscles loosen. The scent of peat and fresh green growth filled my nostrils and reminded me I was home. This was why I couldn't hope for a future with Charlie Nutter. There was something about this farm that felt like it was hardwired into my very soul. I had a bone-deep need to grow things, to nurture and care for them in hopes of watching them flourish.

My dreams for Jackson's Organic Blooms were scary

big, and I needed to be here full-time to achieve them. My family wasn't the only one depending on the success of the business. I had employees who'd invested their own time and energy into getting us where we wanted to go.

As I moved down the rows of seedlings, inspecting and pruning here and there, I thought back to the way Charlie had talked about his own job. He was proud of his work. I could tell by the way he talked about it and defended it. He'd gone to school for it and had presumably found his calling in the company there in Chicago. How could I expect him to give that up for me when I knew Licking Thicket didn't have anything that would come close to the kind of career he wanted?

And why was I trying to solve a problem that didn't exist? It wasn't like I wanted Charlton to move back here... did I? How could I know when I hadn't seen the man in fifteen years?

You know him.

My instincts tried to convince me that a person's character stood the test of time, that the boy I'd admired and wanted to spend time with was the same man I craved today. At least, I *wanted* to believe that.

And if he was the same man, or if my gut could be trusted, I couldn't help but want more from him than a one-night stand or two before he disappeared back to the city for another decade.

The squeal of the greenhouse door opening had me spinning around in time to see Diesel Partridge walk in, backlit against the morning sky. I wondered why he was here instead of with his family, getting ready to stuff his face with mashed potatoes.

"Diesel, hey. Everything okay? Parrish? And Marigold?"

His face softened at the mention of his husband and daughter. "They're fine. Cooking away with Parrish's aunt and uncle since we don't eat until later. Which, ah..." He lifted one tattooed hand to scratch his head. "...is why I'm here. Do you have any sweet potatoes?"

"Sweet potatoes," I repeated.

"Yeah. For, like..." Diesel cleared his throat. "Sweet potato casserole?"

I nodded slowly. "Sure. I grew a bumper crop this year, and we have some in the storage barn. How many do you need?"

"You know." He shrugged. "A... casserole-ish amount. Also, if you happen to have a recipe for sweet potato casserole, that would be helpful."

I tilted my head to look at him. "Did you forget to go to the grocery store?"

He winced. "No, Parrish did all that. It's just that I mixed up his casserole with the casserole I made for the hens, and I accidentally gave the girls the sweet potatoes. Parrish is pretty pissed."

"Your chickens ate marshmallows?" I asked in sudden concern. "That can't be good for them."

He waved his hand in dismissal. "No, no. He hadn't put them on yet. Those... well, those were used as ammo after he discovered what happened. And then, as soon as he started chucking them at me, Marigold thought it was the best thing ever and started throwing them too."

I could picture the scene so clearly that I could barely hold back my laughter. "Tell you what. We'll head over to my sister's place and steal one of her casseroles. Every year at the Stuffin', she cons twelve people into picking up one of Gracie Mawbry's sweet potato casseroles for her so she can have a freezer full for the upcoming year. She'll never notice one's missing, I promise."

I led Diesel over to the side-by-side I'd left by the green-house and gestured for him to hop in the passenger seat. Once we were on the dirt trail to Alana's small house, Diesel turned to me. "You gonna tell me what was up with that big turkey yesterday? Seemed like there's a story there."

I sighed. There was no such thing as privacy in the Thicket. "His name is Charlie Nutter. He used to live here."

Diesel nodded. "No, I know him. Met him last night at the Johnsons' place. Nice guy." He glanced at me. "Hot too."

"Jesus, fuck, Diesel," I snapped, realizing what he was doing. "Who sent you here?"

He held up both hands in surrender. "I'm here for the yams, I swear."

I narrowed my eyes at him, subconsciously grateful muscle memory would get me to Alana's, even if I didn't spend much time looking at the trail. "Did Parrish put you up to this? Or was it Ava?"

His shoulders slumped. "Just give me something, Hunter. Anything. Do you have any idea how seldom I manage to get any scoop? It's like knowing my man's love language and not speaking a word of it."

I snorted. "Charlie and I... we had a misunderstanding. Years ago. And I was still angry. But last night, we talked it through and forgave each other. It's all water under the bridge now. Case closed."

"Mm. I see."

Thankfully, he didn't say anything further. At least for a few minutes.

He shifted toward me and poked a thick finger into my

shoulder. "But like... what if the case was open? What if it was a different case? What if it was a sexy case that could suck your dick?"

"Diesel Partridge!" I stared at him. "What the fuck?"

He shrugged. "It's just... Charlie asked about you. Last night. He was real concerned when Alana said you might be sick—and I mean, lasering-us-all-with-his-eyeballs-for-abandoning-you concerned. Like, if Alana hadn't been giving us all the same laser eyeballs telling us to keep our mouths shut, some of us might have actually gone to check on you. So... I like him for you, is what I'm saying. If he was that concerned about you before you'd even settled your differences, he must care about you a lot. And he's good people—a bunch of us were sitting around the fire pit, and he talked with us for hours. He fits around here."

Diesel sounded sincere, but I knew a matchmaking rat when I saw one.

"And so you just thought you'd come over here with some sweet potato excuse and tell me all that, huh? Don't lie to me, Partridge. Was Cindy Ann in on this?" It suddenly occurred to me that Cindy Ann Johnson, Katie-Bird Nutter, and Lurleen Jackson had all been at the party last night too. The Thicket Matchmaking Mafia, left unsupervised.

Diesel's eyes flared wide. "N-no! No, I swear. It was Parrish. He has a big heart and wants everyone to have... well, to have what we have."

The big guy's cheeks turned pink, and I groaned. "Don't weaponize that blush, Diesel. It's lethal."

He grinned hopefully. "Give me something to take back to Parrish. Pretty please? I really did fuck up his favorite Thanksgiving dish. I swear."

I knew better than to kiss and tell in this tiny town. That wouldn't be fair to Charlie. But I could give him something. Something that could maybe possibly work its way around the Thicket's grapevine in a way that offered Charlie a little softball of an idea.

"Okay, fine. I like him. I might even *like* him, like him. There, you happy? I may or may not have fantasized about raising chicks with him, alright? Now, stop asking questions and follow me. We have to be stealthy about this, or Alana will lose her shit."

He grabbed my arm before I could escape the side-by-side. "Wait. You think... you think he'd want to raise chicks?" There was a gleam in his eyes. "We could form like... a club or something."

I stared at him. "Yes, Diesel. Gays with Chicks. Start drawing up the bylaws."

He nodded absently while his brain went in directions I didn't even want to know about. "Gays with Chicks," he murmured. "Not sure that sounds right."

I yanked my arm from his grip and hopped out. "Come on. Let's steal some casserole."

———

Seven hours later, I never wanted to see another potato or potato-based product in my life. I groaned and patted my belly gently, silently apologizing to it for the day's abuse. "Can't move."

My dad grunted. "Shouldn't have had the whipped cream on the pie. That was the tipping point."

My mom scoffed. "Sure, babe. It was the whipped cream that did you in. Mmhm."

Alana turned off the kitchen sink and whipped her head around to pierce me with an accusatory stare. "What did you do?"

"Uh... ate too much?" I looked around to see if anyone else understood what had come over her.

"I just had one of my *feelings*," she said. "And I know you did something."

I tried not to remember the casserole caper from earlier. My sister's supposed mental telepathy powers were stronger if there were images in the brain she was attempting to breach. "I promise I ate too much food. Oh! And I also fed the leftover drumstick to Butterbean. Sorry."

My parents gasped. Aunt Connie sighed with disappointment. "That's how it starts."

Dad pointed a finger at me. "You gave it to the dog? Y'know I would have eaten that tomorrow."

I held back a laugh. "No. You would have said you were going to eat it, and then you would have seen Mom make a giant turkey sandwich with stuffing and cranberry sauce, and you would have asked her to make you one, leaving the poor drumstick to get repeatedly overlooked until it went off."

Dad let out a resigned sigh. "It's the only time of year you can get that sandwich."

Aunt Connie sighed again. "Still. Giving a drumstick to the dog? Who raised you? Do you have any idea how much that drumstick cost?"

Mom, Dad, Alana, and I exchanged guilty glances, but no one had the guts to tell Aunt Connie Mom had gotten it for two dollars with her coupons. Aunt Connie and my mother had a years-long coupon war going on, and sometimes the savings were so good you just had to keep it to yourself to keep the peace. This was definitely one of those situations.

Alana cleared her throat and turned to me. "Stop changing the subject. You did something, Hunter Jackson."

Her face lit up. "Hold on... hold *on*. You hooked up with Junior Nutter! Oh my God, you did. Look at your cheeks! They're like my old Raggedy Ann doll with the red patches. Tell me everything!"

The image of Charlie's red lips stretched tight around my cock flashed into my mind. "Ohhhh, oh, no. Nooo, absolutely not. Nothing to tell, really. Ab-so-lute-ly noth-ing."

Everyone stared at me, but it was my dad who whistled low under his breath. "Who knew you were such a terrible liar? You beat me all the time at poker. How is that possible?"

I got up and busied myself with checking the leftovers to make sure they were properly stored. Improperly stored leftovers were the single biggest cause of post-Thanksgiving Day food poisoning.

At least, I assumed that was the case. It sounded good anyway.

Mom came up behind me and pulled the containers from my hands to return them to the fridge. Once she closed the refrigerator door, she turned me around and clasped my upper arms.

"Hunter Briggs Jackson," she said. Instead of the angry tone she usually used when she full-named me, this time, it was the tender, loving tone that made me feel like a little boy who was about to get one of Lurleen's Life Lessons.

"Lurleen Calhoun Davenport Jackson," I parroted, but she ignored it.

"I think you're doing the right thing to guard your heart and reject Junior. He's not from around here."

I frowned. That was not at all what I'd expected her to say. "He's literally from the Thicket," I corrected. "And his name is Charlie."

"You know what I mean. He's not sticking around. His

people never do." She sniffed, punctuating the vague reference to Charlie's father, who'd done the unthinkable: slept with a country music star's gorgeous young daughter and had the audacity to profit off it. "So it's all for the best that you keep that boy at arm's length. Ignore his pushy come-ons or whatever it is he's doing, and keep your eyes on your own page. Keep your vehicle in your own lane and your eyes on the road."

She was losing me with her metaphors.

"I'm... I'm not driving with him. Or whatever," I said. "I know he's going back to Chicago. I know that."

She nodded. "Good. That's all I wanted to be sure of. Because he's a nice boy, but upon further reflection, I've realized he's not for you. Not at *all*. Definitely, definitely not. In fact, I would be... I would be horrified and appalled if you ended up with him. I would... I would never speak to you again."

"You promise?" I teased.

My mother batted my shoulder. "I'm serious, Hunter. *Deadly* serious."

"Uh-huh." I tilted my head to look at her. "Reverse psychology's not your usual move."

She patted her perfect hair nervously. "I... I don't know what you could mean. I'm just looking out for you, baby."

"And I appreciate that," I agreed. "Please pass my thanks on to Ms. Nutter, too, when you're texting her later."

Her shoulders slumped. "Katie-Bird and I *told* Cindy Ann this would never work," she muttered. "But Cindy Ann's got an undeniable matchmaking track record, so I had to give it a whirl."

"I understand." I leaned forward to give her a hug. "Thanks for looking out for me, Mom. I appreciate it." I pulled back and met her eyes. "And I'm glad you like Charlie. He's a good man."

She watched me warily. "You're not still holding a grudge about Dolly, are you?"

"No. We, ah…" I glanced behind her at Alana, who was showing Aunt Connie some photos on her phone. "We talked, and it turns out he had a good reason for doing what he did. I'm over it, just like you and Dad said I should be."

She pressed her lips together, clearly dying to ask for an explanation, but before she could, I pressed a kiss to her cheek. "I'm going to head home. Thanks for everything. The food was amazing, as usual."

"You going to take some of these leftovers?"

"Nah, I'll come by and eat them here. I know where you live," I said with a wink.

I waved goodbye to everyone else before slipping out the door and heading back to my place.

It was already nine o'clock, but I hoped Charlie was still up for a visit. I pulled my phone out and shot him a text.

Hunter: *I'm home. Stop by if you're free.*

I entered the house and spent a few minutes cleaning up. I changed the sheets, swapped out fresh towels for my damp ones, and made sure the porch light was on. By eleven, he still hadn't responded. At midnight, I had to face the fact that he wasn't coming. No one would show up at someone's place after midnight without at least texting first.

I shuffled over to the front door and flicked off the porch light before turning the dead bolt. Then, I turned off the kitchen light and the lamps in the living room before heading to my bedroom to try and get some sleep. I told myself I wasn't disappointed. After all, he'd be leaving in a few short days anyway, and I knew it. Better that I didn't get too attached.

But I wasn't sure I believed it.

I was just drifting off to sleep when a loud banging woke me up with a start. I knocked my head on the bedside table rolling out of bed, still half dozing.

"Wait, wait," I yelled, simply to stop the banging. "I'm coming." I turned on the porch light and unbolted the door.

Charlie stood on the other side with winter-bright eyes and puffs of white vapor coming out of his mouth like he was out of breath. "Sorry I'm late," he said. His expression made it clear he was unsure of his reception.

I rubbed the sore spot on my head while I tried to get my thoughts in order. "No, that's... it's..."

"Fuck, are you hurt? Again?" He knocked my hand out of the way and began palpating my skull again. Before we could start another comedy of errors, I stopped him.

"I was almost asleep when you knocked, and I bumped my head on the bedside table."

His forehead crinkled. "Babe... I am concerned about your balance. I think you should see someone about repeated blows to the head."

It wasn't the first time he'd called me babe, but it set off a sparkler of excitement in my gut that made me lunge for him. "Get in here," I said before kissing the breath from him and pulling him backward into the house.

Chapter Eleven

Charlton

I FELT terrible for showing up so late, but the minute Hunter grabbed me and pulled me into the house, I realized just how badly I needed this. Had he turned me away, I might have had to try my hand at breaking and entering.

"Sorry I'm late," I said between kisses and nips. "Family stuff, you know?"

He grunted his understanding but didn't take his mouth off me to vocalize it. I let myself relax into the impromptu make-out session for several minutes before I realized I hadn't even wished him a happy Thanksgiving.

I pulled back and cupped his face. "Hey. How was your day?"

Hunter wrapped his arms around me and pulled me closer. "Good. Really good. Lots to be thankful for. But I'm really glad it's over so I can do this." He arched his back, and our cocks shifted against each other through our clothes.

"Same," I groaned. "Hard same. Take me to—"

A shrill *quack, quack* cut off the rest of my demand, and Hunter and I froze in place.

"What the hell?" he demanded against my lips.

I winced. "That's my mom's text notification." I pulled away from his embrace to dig my phone out of my pocket. "Sorry! *Sorry.* But I don't think she'd text me at this hour unless it was an emergency—" I swiped the screen.

Mom: *Strangest thing, Charlton! I went to the bunk room a little while ago to say goodnight to my precious son and ask what he was chatting about with Cousin Buck earlier, only to find he'd (gasp!) LEFT without a single word to anyone!*
Mom: *But then I realized you're probably out doing NICE deeds for our neighbors—say, for example, that adorable Hunter Jackson?—in honor of the holiday. Right, sweetheart?*
Mom: *I'm so proud! I can't wait to brag on you to Lurleen and Cindy Ann and Amos and Emmaline and... well, everyone! lol.*
Mom: *Just remember you haven't won the bet yet, kiddo. Love you!*

I squeezed my eyes shut and muttered a succinct "Fuck."

"What?" Hunter asked, instantly concerned. "Is she okay? Is it Amos? Do you need to get home?"

"No! Hell no. I may never go back to Amos's again." I turned the screen so Hunter could read the messages.

"I don't get it," he said after a moment. "What bet? What nice deeds?"

With a sigh, I explained about the niceness bet I'd been trying to win... and how my mom seemed to be playing dirty.

I'd expected Hunter to roll his eyes or even to be annoyed that so many Thicketeers were going to know our business. Laughing so hard his head went back and his eyes watered was not even in my top five anticipated reactions... but apparently, it should have been.

"Wait. Wait, wait, wait," he gasped out. "So you're telling me that the reason you took part in the Biddin', the reason you didn't throw the turkey costume in my face yesterday... was so you could win a bet with your mom?"

"Kinda. At first. Yeah." I folded my arms over my chest as he doubled over again. "It's not that funny. It's the *Waldorf* spa, Hunter. It costs a billion dollars. And my mother is a wonderful woman in many ways, but if you think she's the kind of mom who wouldn't make me pay up —and mention her win at every opportunity for the rest of my life—you're wrong."

"Oh, I'm very familiar with exactly that kind of mom, babe. Our mothers are peas in a pod," Hunter said. His eyes took on a calculating look. "I'm guessing your mom doesn't know about our conversation at the event barn yesterday, then, hmm?"

"No." I frowned. "Why would she?"

"No reason. Except, thinking back, I'm not sure you were entirely..." He adopted a sorrowful expression and sighed pitifully. "...nice."

For once, I recognized the teasing light in his eyes for what it was and refused to be conned. I closed the distance between us with a single step and poked him lightly in the stomach. "Excuse you. I was every bit as nice as *you* were, Hunter Jackson."

"See?" he said plaintively. "I feel very attacked." He grabbed my hand and used it to pull me against him, then grinned down at me. "And, just to say, *I'm* not the one who has a niceness bet to win... or *lose*. So."

I shook my head slowly, torn between laughter and outrage. How the hell could someone so annoying be so damn adorable? And why the hell did I like it so damn much? When had being teased by Hunter Jackson started to feel as necessary as coffee, or oxygen, or sunshine, like the sort of thing I didn't want to live without?

I lifted an eyebrow. "You are *not* telling my mother I was cranky," I warned.

"No?" Hunter gently pushed me back against his front door and blocked me in with his body. "I'm sure if you were *extra* nice right now, it would... help me forget."

Heat washed down my spine and made me suck in a breath. "That *is* what I'm here for," I reminded him breathlessly. "That's what we were in the middle of doing when we were rudely interrupted." I nipped him lightly on the chin. "I can be extra, *extra* nice."

Hunter's breath hitched in a gratifying way. "Extra, *extra* nice? Because I have an idea, but you might not like it..."

"Anything," I said rashly, surprised to find that I meant it. "I trust you." Hunter would never hurt me.

"Fuck, Charlie. So sweet," he sighed into the sensitive skin right below my ear. I shivered, my hips tilting up to meet his... and found nothing but air since Hunter stepped back at precisely that moment and held out a hand. "Let's talk."

I blinked. "T-talk," I repeated. Then, in a higher pitch, "You want to *talk*? I don't suppose that's a... a quaint Thicket euphemism for things that don't involve talking at all?"

"Nope." He led me over to his sofa and dropped down into the seat. "It's a thing people do when they like each other. When they're friends as well as... whatever else they might be." He pulled me down to sit beside him and added in a lower voice, "When they know they have all night to do anything and *everything* else they might want. It's foreplay."

I swallowed hard. This was an excellent point, and I couldn't argue with it. But also, "Just to be clear, after talky time is over, then..."

"Then I'll be extra nice to *you*." Hunter's grin was dirty, molten perfection. "And that *is* a euphemism, babe."

I let out a shuddery breath and gripped his hand tightly. "Fine. I can talk. Heck, half my life is talking. I can talk for hours. That's... easy peasy." I stared at him for a long moment, but the only thoughts in my head were X-rated and far better suited to action than words. "What should we talk about?"

Hunter sank back into the cushion, pushing his knee against mine. "Start with this: How was your day, Charlton? How'd it go with your family? Was it overwhelming? Was it fun? Were you glad you came back?"

I blew out a breath. "It was... nice?" I winced, and Hunter chuckled. "No, seriously, though, it was overwhelming *and* fun. It was special. Made me realize I shouldn't have waited so long to come home, but also that maybe..." I bit my lip, and Hunter watched patiently as I figured out how I was feeling. "Maybe I needed to stay away as long as I did so I could see it more clearly on this visit. If I'd come home more often, I wonder if the changes around here would have been too subtle for me to notice."

"Changes?" Hunter cocked his head curiously. "I feel like the Thicket's mostly the same it's always been."

"It's definitely not. Don't get me wrong, plenty of things haven't changed. But there's so much more business here, more diversity, more open-mindedness. The town is thriving. When we were at the Stuffin' yesterday, I couldn't believe how packed all the storefronts were with shops and businesses. Don't you remember when we were in elementary school and half of those buildings were either falling down or empty? I noticed Quinn's wedding planning showroom—that's not something the Thicket used to be able to support. And the fact you and your sister can open up an event space in addition to the community center and expect it to book up is something you wouldn't have been able to do back then either."

"I guess that's true." He toyed with my fingers as he thought about what I was saying. "Some large companies bought up land just outside of town, and that brought a lot of new people in from Nashville and Knoxville... all over the world, really. And now that more city companies are letting employees work from home, we have people who've moved here from Atlanta and Chicago just to take advantage of the low cost of living and the slower pace of life. Brooks's husband is from LA, I think, and Brooks moved back from New York."

"Brooks's *artist* husband," I said pointedly. "Who creates and displays his art right here in the Thicket?"

Hunter grinned. "You met Mal, huh?"

"I did... and felt like an asshole for what I said yesterday afternoon." I shook my head. "I must've sounded like such a know-it-all, telling you what opportunities a person can and can't have around here."

"Eh. I might've thought so yesterday, but if we're being honest..." He scratched his beard. "I was at least as much of an asshole as you were. I expected you to come back from Chicago and look down on everything here. I was being defensive on behalf of this little town." His mouth quirked up. "And myself."

"You weren't too far wrong, though," I admitted, though it pained me. "I expected to feel that way—*did* feel it when I first drove through town— but there's something attractive about living in a place where people know you, where you recognize your neighbors at the grocery store and know you can call on someone nearby when you need help." I took a deep breath. "You made a smart choice, staying in the Thicket. Building your business here."

"Yeah?" Hunter's face flushed pink with embarrassed pleasure today instead of anger. "I mean, I agree. Clearly. But what I *didn't* say yesterday is that having big dreams in a small town comes with certain challenges." His fingers traced my palm as if memorizing the lines there. "You don't just get to follow a path anyone else has laid out, you have to break every trail yourself. People, even my own family, wonder why I'm not satisfied supplying the Thicket area or at least Middle Tennessee. 'Why the quest for organic houseplant world-domination, Hunter?'" He shook his head, a rueful half-smile on his face. "And that's not even considering how, *logistics-and-distribution-wise*, it's tough running a business when you're a long drive down a dusty road from your customers." He knocked his shoulder into mine.

"Oh, well, now you're speaking my language." I drew my legs up onto the sofa and faced him. "So, are you mostly trucking your plants to a local distributor at this point? Because overland shipping is convenient but limiting, as you're finding out, and air cargo isn't always as expensive as you'd think, depending on where you'd be shipping things, especially when there's that FBO outside town. I know there are special considerations since the plants have to be kept alive and whatnot, but have you considered..."

I sketched out some of the more obvious transportation and distribution options he might have based on what little I knew about his business goals and the products he was selling. I got so into it that it took me a minute—or possibly more—to notice that Hunter's eyes had gone glassy and his flush hadn't gone away.

"Shit. I lost you, didn't I?" Now it was my turn to blush. "I'm sorry. That was a lot of jargon to throw around when you're probably still in the midst of a post-turkey tryptophan coma." Hunter didn't reply, and my face went hotter. "And, double shit, you didn't even ask me for help, did you? I did that thing where I just jumped right in to provide solutions when you were maybe only venting about the problem. I got excited, I guess, and—*mmmph!*"

I broke off when Hunter grabbed my jaw in one hand and kissed me with hot, thorough possession.

"Are you kidding me right now?" he whispered against my lips. "Charlton Nutter, you can be as excited as you want about my business. I can't believe I didn't ask you before. You're a logistics and distribution genius."

"I, uh... am I?" I wondered. Since I couldn't remember my own name, I would have to take his word for it. "Okay."

"Nobody ever... I mean, I never feel like I can talk to people about this." He sat back, keeping one of my hands firmly in his, and ran his other hand through his hair. "The hardest part about running your own business is that you do it all yourself. I have some pretty great employees, and folks in town are as supportive as they can be, but I'm the guy in charge. The toilet in the office breaks, it's on me. We get hit with powdery mildew? On me. Tish is out for six weeks because she tweaked her knee while building a tree fort for her grandkids and needs to make sure she's still getting paid? I mean, technically, that's on the benefits contractor I pay, but making sure they're doing what needs to be done? On me. And figuring out a better supply chain system so our business can level up is on me too, except I hadn't gotten there yet because I was too busy dealing with all the other shit. You've given me a lot to think about in five minutes."

"Really?" I couldn't stop grinning.

Hunter shook his head wonderingly. "*Really*, he asks. Of course, really! No wonder you're vice president of whatever-the-fuck company you work for. Don't suppose y'all would be willing to take on a logistics side hustle for a houseplant farmer, huh?" he joked. "Don't they need plants in industrial kitchens?"

"Ha. I think yesterday we covered the fact that I have no idea *what* people need in industrial kitchens," I said dryly.

And if it hadn't already become clear to me why that was a problem, it certainly would have after this conversation. No promotion I'd ever gotten had made me as genuinely satisfied as seeing Hunter Jackson's happiness and feeling like my ideas might help ease the burdens of his business. Hunter was right—I'd missed getting involved. I'd missed helping people. I'd let my need for stability grow until it choked out an important part of my nature. No wonder I felt unfulfilled at my job.

"Besides," I went on lightly, "I thought we agreed that you preferred the term *organic nursery owner*. Owner of the largest houseplant supplier in Middle Tennessee, I believe you said?"

"Oh. Well." Hunter caught my eye and gave me a flirty grin that did things to my stomach. "When I'm trying to impress a hot guy, sure."

A bubble of laughter escaped me. "Puh-lease. Don't pretend to be all modest now, Jackson. Just today, my cousin Eulalia was raving today about Emmaline's Boston fern as we were sitting down for pecan pie. *Oh my gawwwd, it's so lusssshhhh, Emmaline! How'd y'all get it to doooo thaaat?*" I snickered a little at my own impression of Eulalia's deep drawl. "Emmaline told her, proud as a peacock, that the secret was getting a Jackson's Organic Blooms plant. She said they're prized all over the Thicket. Every household has at least one, like it's a status symbol."

"Everyone's been really supportive."

"Because they know you, and they care." I pushed his knee gently. "Like I was saying before. They want to help."

"That's true." Hunter scrunched up his face. "Of course, those same helpful neighbors also have their noses *permanently* inserted in your business. If you think too hard about how many people spent their holiday discussing The Great Turkey Incident Part Two: Hunter's Revenge or will spend their Black Friday dishing about Part Three: The Turkey Niceness Bet, you'd run screaming to the airport and put yourself on the standby list."

"Probably." I laughed softly and leaned against Hunter's side so I could run my fingertips through his beard and tug on it a little. "But... life in the city isn't perfect either. It's too far in the other direction sometimes. Don't get me wrong, I have good friends—my best friend, Seamus, is amazing—but life there feels more transient. Sometimes I make friends, and then they move away to pursue another job opportunity, or they wind up dating someone new and I never see them again. It was nice last night to see several gay couples all hanging out together at Brooks's parents' house, super chill and settled. We drank and laughed around a fire pit. It was the kind of life I dreamed about when I was a kid. I just... I never really thought I could have that here in the Thicket since I wasn't straight, you know?"

Understanding warmed Hunter's gaze. "Of course I know. I grew up gay here too, Charlie. Sounds like maybe you figured out your sexuality before I did if you knew you were gay before you left—I hadn't quite cottoned on at that point—but once I did, well... as much as I love the Thicket and wanted to stay here, there were times when I wondered if I *could*. Like, would living here mean I could never hook up with anyone, much less settle down someday? If I had to make that trade, could I? One time, I went to Atlanta Pride and had so much fun with so many hot guys I spent the whole drive home fantasizing about what it would be like to live there." He grinned. "Of course, I was over it long before I hit the town limits because I wanted *this* more." He nodded toward the farmland outside his house. "And it was a moot point anyway since the gay population of the Thicket is... let's say *robust*. But I do understand why living here isn't for everyone. It's not as easy as I made it out to be, and there's no one right choice. That's what I would have said yesterday... if I were being *nice*."

Hunter's voice was low and earnest, and it felt like the most natural thing in the world for me to shift a little closer, until my knees were practically in his lap, just so I could feel his warmth and breathe in the scent of him.

This was the conversation we could have had in the event barn the day before if there hadn't been so many misunderstandings, so much hurt and defensiveness, between us. It was more than just a prelude to sex, more than just foreplay. It was *belonging* on a whole other level, and it was no hardship whatsoever...

At least until the part where Hunter mentioned his sex-filled Pride weekend.

My reaction was as unattractive as it was irrational—I'd never been jealous about anyone I'd dated, and Hunter and I weren't even dating, for heaven's sake—but I couldn't deny the little twinge somewhere right below my ribcage, like a discordant note in an otherwise peaceful tune.

"So do you... have you... I mean, you've ended up finding people. Here. To, ah..." I cleared my throat.

Hunter's eyes got bigger with every stumble over my words. "What are you asking me, Charlton Heston?"

I groaned and rubbed my face with my hand before pinning him with a look. "Never. Mind."

His laugh was warm and rumbling, and he squeezed my fingers tight. "I haven't been a chaste maiden, if that's what you're asking, and no, I haven't hooked up with anyone in your family tree, so don't even ask me about your cousin Elmer. I've had hookups here and there and a few weekend trips to places that had a bigger selection, but I've only really dated one guy seriously."

"Oh?" Curiosity curdled in my stomach. I wasn't sure if I wanted to know. "Who?"

"College boyfriend. I went to UT for Horticulture Science and Organic Production. Don't know if I told you that," he explained. "Anyway, Lane—or I guess he's Dr. Desmond now—was another ag student. Pre-vet studies. Really nice guy. Smart too. Went on to veterinary school at University of Georgia and ended up staying on to teach, but I think he might be ready to move into private practice. I keep telling him he should move to the Thicket, but—"

"I don't care about his resume, Hunter. Jesus," I snapped. Instantly, I felt my face go hot. "Erm. Sorry," I added quickly. "I just, uh... I just meant... How long were you together?"

Hunter's lips twitched like he knew exactly why I was snappish. "Two and a half years?" He shifted toward me. "Honestly, I look back on it and wonder if I just wanted to play house with someone. On paper, we worked fine. We went grocery shopping together and grilled out. We stayed in on Friday nights and watched movies together in bed like an old married couple. We had a ton in common. And you know, I don't think we ever really fought," he added thoughtfully. "Not once."

"Delightful." I gritted my teeth. "Really. That's... great. So why'd you break up? I mean, clearly, you're still in touch since you're trying to get him to move here." I tried not to dwell on the fact that Hunter and I had done almost nothing *but* fight since I'd gotten back to the Thicket or that he hadn't tried to persuade *me* to move here even once.

I failed on both fronts.

Hunter's lips curved into a delectable grin. "We broke up because I tried to get him to wear a turkey costume once, and he looked awful in it."

For a split second, I thought he was being serious. When I realized he was teasing me *yet again*, I socked him in the shoulder. "Be serious. Why didn't it work out?"

Hunter shrugged. "I don't know, Charlie. We were babies? We were too alike? We wanted different things? He had the most annoying habit of correcting people who ended a sentence with a preposition. I always wondered how he could have survived going to school in Georgia and Tennessee with this particular affliction, but apparently, he made it."

"*Hmph.* He sounds like a pretentious ass."

Hunter grinned. "I know. But he really isn't. He just gets insecure, and it comes out in a pedantic way. None of us are perfect. What about you?"

"Definitely not perfect. But I try not to correct people's grammar," I said, trying to win at least one point from the successful and most likely hot veterinarian.

Hunter laughed and wrapped one large, warm arm around my shoulder, pulling me down into his side. "I meant *dating*, babe. Have you ever dated anyone seriously?"

"Oh." I thought about it for a long moment, snuggling deeper into his embrace. "I've dated a few people long enough to consider it a relationship. I dated one guy for about a year. We actually moved in together in the city to save on rent, *then* we started dating. Zero out of ten stars, do not recommend."

"Don't date your sexy roommate? Are you sure?" Hunter demanded, pulling away to give me an affronted look. "Porn has steered me so wrong."

I snickered. "He was a nice enough guy. I enjoyed going out with him because we liked a lot of the same things. We ran together along the waterfront when the weather was nice, and we worked out at the gym together when it wasn't. He liked seeing shows and concerts during a time I was trying to experience as much of the city as possible. It was good for that time and place in my life, but neither of us had strong enough feelings to... renew the lease." I shot him a wink. "We still keep in touch and catch a show together from time to time. He's in a serious relationship now with an actor, so he gets good last-minute seats."

Hunter nodded easily, his thumb stroking up and down my bicep through my sweater in a way that made me want to stretch out like a cat and jump his bones at the same time. But that discordant note was still there, making it hard to sink into the close, relaxing vibe. I felt... awkward. And I finally realized that awkwardness was because we were talking *around* what I really wanted to know:

How did Hunter Jackson feel about *me*?

Because I was falling for him hard and fast, and I wasn't quite sure I'd packed a parachute.

On the one hand, this felt normal. Inevitable. He'd been my very first crush, after all. But this bout was infinitely worse, like one of those tropical fevers you sometimes read about that lay dormant for years only to come back with a vengeance. *I'm sorry, Mr. Nutter, but once you've contracted Hunter Jackson Fever, there is no cure.*

"Charlie? Y'okay?" Hunter asked when the silence had gone on a bit too long.

Yes. Great. Just... comparing my feelings for you to a plague.

"Fine," I assured him. I pulled his hand up to kiss it. "Were you in love with Lane?"

He shook his head slowly. "I don't think so. You?"

"I've never even met the man." I waited for him to roll his eyes before I responded seriously. "No, never. Not... not... no." Part of me wanted to say "not yet" or "not with anyone other than you," but I knew this wasn't the time. Besides, I wasn't actually in love with Hunter... yet, and the last thing I wanted to do was scare him off.

But when I leaned forward to kiss him and his responding kiss was heartbreakingly tender and sweet, I realized the words were irrelevant. As we moved together, our bodies—our fingertips and mouths and the gentle brush of our skin—expressed the newly emerging feelings we had for each other.

Hunter pulled away, and for a heartbeat, his eyes met mine. "Talky time is over."

Chapter Twelve

Hunter

ONCE WE GOT to the bedroom, we took our time peeling the clothes off each other and exploring each other's bodies with touches and tongues until I wanted to cry with the overwhelming feelings I had for him. Our eyes locked and held for long moments. Unspoken words of affection, disbelief, relief, and celebration moved between us, crowding out any shred of worry or doubt.

After fifteen years of anger and misunderstandings, we were finally, impossibly, inevitably together, and the look in his eyes was all the proof I needed that we were on the same page.

This was something real, something with hope and possibility.

This was a beginning.

"Mine," Charlie breathed before kissing the apple of my cheek and moving to kiss in front of my ear, then underneath it. Goose bumps prickled on my skin. "Please, mine."

"*Yes.*" The word was so soft I wasn't sure I'd actually said it out loud. But the expression in his eyes, of surprise and joy, was unmistakable.

Charlie lay over me on the bed, our bare bodies fitting together perfectly. "Can I—"

"Yes," I said again. "Yes, please. God, yes."

I gestured to the bedside table, where he found lube and condoms. He used the lube to begin to prep me with his fingers, moving my legs apart and teasing my cock with his mouth at the same time. I ran my fingers into his hair as he worked, and I couldn't hold in the noises he brought out in me.

When I couldn't possibly be more ready, he rolled on the condom and slicked the tip before crawling over me again and pressing my legs back. "You okay?"

I was already blissed-out, hard and flushed with desire. The man on top of me was truly stunning, and my stomach clenched with a sense of unreality.

Me and Charlie Nutter. Together. *Amazing*.

I smiled and nodded before pulling Charlie closer. He positioned himself at my entrance and began to press inside.

The tight stretch of his cock made my eyes roll back. I groaned as he continued moving forward.

I clutched his hips, encouraging him to keep going. The fullness was almost unbearable until he pressed up against just the right spot. It was too good, too fucking incredible, and I wondered if I'd be able to hold on long enough to make it good for him too.

As soon as he was as deep inside of me as he could go, I groaned and arched up, rubbing my dripping cock against his stomach. His dark eyes held mine as he reached down to stroke me and began to drag himself in and out of my body.

My eyes slid closed in pleasure as I groaned again. Pretty sure I murmured words of incredulity at his body and the way it made me feel, but I wasn't quite all there. This joining, this connection with him... it was transformative. It shook something inside of me until it settled deep and still where it was always meant to be.

I didn't want it to end.

I'd told Charlie that I'd never been in love before, and I hadn't, so I didn't exactly know what all-the-way-in-love was supposed to feel like. But in that moment, I thought maybe it would feel like *this*. Like being linked to someone who challenged and excited you, who wanted and appreciated you, who opened your mind and your heart when you'd never realized they were closed. Like wanting to make someone else happy so you could revel in their pleasure and, in doing so, achieve your own. Like you were half of a larger whole but also more authentically and totally yourself than you'd ever been.

I watched Charlie thrust in and out of me. With his brows furrowed in concentration, his hair damp around the edges, and his pulse flickering unsteadily in his neck, he was the absolute most beautiful thing I'd ever laid eyes on.

My fingers tightened on his hips a split second before I cried out my release. I watched with bleary eyes as he shuddered above me, but I was too out of it to do more other than smile stupidly.

Charlie reached down to remove the condom before falling next to me on the bed. We both lay there, attempting to catch our breath, when I turned to face him. "Stay. Please."

I could tell he was unsure of my meaning, whether it was a teasing request for round two or a serious invitation.

I... wasn't entirely sure either. I didn't know what was right or fair to ask for. What he wanted. What he *needed*. All I knew was what I wanted—as much of Charlton Nutter as I could get.

"Please," I repeated, making sure he understood there was nothing but honest entreaty in my tone.

My heart pounded, and my stomach churned with uncharacteristic nerves. Normally when I wanted something, I put my head down and found a way to get it, but I had a feeling stubbornness wasn't going to work here. Charlie and I had just had sex... and not the casual kind. We'd *made love*—something one should definitely never do with a partner who lived several hundred miles away and probably had no interest in making a drastic life change.

He reached out to run his fingers through my hair, and his dark eyes softened. "I would have even if you hadn't invited me," he admitted before leaning over to press a soft kiss to my lips.

I gloried in the simple touch and told myself that there'd be time to deal with the fallout of this *tomorrow*. In the meantime, I could enjoy both Charlie's body and his company.

It was funny how, in one short day, Charlie had gone from being a person I thought I couldn't stand to being... well, a person I craved spending time with. Like now that all the bricks of anger and misunderstanding I'd spent fifteen years stacking between us were gone, the sweet, understanding friend I'd thought I'd lost was back... and exponentially sexier and more fun to be with than ever. Talking with him tonight had started out as foreplay, but hearing his thoughts on everything from the Thicket to my business had given me a fresh perspective on my own life that made me more appreciative of the things I had.

Once we were cleaned up and back in bed, I snuggled up next to him as close as I could get, resting my cheek on his chest. I wanted to tell him I was falling for him, that I wanted him more than just for sex.

That I wanted him to *stay*.

Instead, I bit the bullet and asked, "When do you head back to Chicago?"

His fingers, which had been stroking the hair at the nape of my neck, twitched slightly. "Sunday afternoon."

"Mm. Busiest travel day of the year," I murmured. "You could always... I dunno... change to Monday or whatever. Just to avoid the crush."

"Yeah... maybe." Charlie sounded so noncommittal my heart sank.

"Right," I said softly. "Well, no pressure."

"It's not that I don't want more time here..." he explained in a rush. "But I just got promoted to VP a couple months ago, and my boss only approved my time off this week because I have six weeks of unused vacation."

My fingertips dragged haphazard patterns across his chest as I considered this. Last time I'd talked to him about his job, it hadn't gone over so well, but lots of things had changed since then... for me, at least. I hoped the same was true for him.

"Charlie, you know that's not healthy, right?" I began gently. "You deserve to have a life outside of work. And I'm not talking shit about your career. I get it now—"

He dropped a kiss on the top of my head. "I know."

"—I'm just saying there are other jobs in your field, right? Maybe even ones in, uh... places besides Chicago?" I couldn't bring myself to actually suggest him moving back to Tennessee, though everything inside of me wanted to.

"Funny you should say that." Charlie's arm tightened around my shoulder. "I spent a long time talking to my cousin Buck earlier today. He said he might have a position for me."

I popped my head up and stared at him. "Here in the

Thicket? That would be... that's..." I took a breath. "How would you feel about that?"

His eyes warmed as he reached up to caress my cheek. "I think I'd like a change. For a lot of reasons." We locked eyes, and for a split second, I thought I had a chance at my happily ever after. But then he continued. "But the job he suggested would never work."

I felt like I'd been sucker punched. "No? I mean... no. Right."

"For one thing, Buck is... well, he's Buck," Charlie said, as though this were self-explanatory, and for anyone who knew Buck, I supposed it was. Buck was a bit of a hot mess —equal parts brilliant and ridiculous, well-meaning and annoying since it was impossible to tell if the things he said were actually true or merely what he'd convinced himself was true.

"Plus," Charlie went on, "the job he's talking about would be working for his new video game company—he's come up with a new game *so big and hard, the whole world'll stop playing with their Horns and pay attention, mark my words, Junior!*" He rolled his eyes.

"Is that even possible?" I was vaguely appalled by the idea. I'd never been a gamer, but from what I'd seen, Horn of Glory was already an addictive, technicolor, Narnia-like acid trip.

"That's what Buck says, and given what he's already created, it's not out of the realm of possibility." Charlie hesitated. "The thing is, I know nothing about the video game business, but it seems to me that taking a role at a multinational organization that's anticipating meteoric growth isn't any closer to my ideal job than the one I have now. I'd still end up managing managers who'd be managing teams. I still wouldn't get any kind of personal interaction. I'd still be crazy busy and working constantly. So... that would be stupid and shortsighted. Right?"

"Yeah. I... I guess it would." I exhaled and settled back down against his chest for a long minute while his heart beat a rapid cadence against my ear.

A selfish part of me wanted to convince him to take Buck's job anyway—Charlie's current job wasn't perfect either, and at least this way, we could be together—but even if it was possible to persuade him, I knew it wouldn't be fair.

Since I was a kid, I'd dreamed of a future in the Thicket: of starting a business, of falling in love, of raising a family and watching them thrive. The what and the where of that dream had never really been in doubt for me. Now I knew *who* I wanted to share the dream with too, which was both terrifying and amazing, but it didn't feel like a cataclysmic shift so much as a crucial puzzle piece slotting into place to finally reveal a clear picture.

For nearly as long, though, Charlie had actively avoided dreaming of a future here in this small town, let alone with me. While I hoped that had changed a little in the last couple of days, it wasn't fair to expect him to be on the same page I was yet. Moving to the Thicket would mean chucking his whole fancy life out the window, and who'd take that kind of risk on the basis of a winning bet, two days of Thicket turkey shenanigans, and a couple of rounds of truly incredible sex?

Not the stability-loving man I was falling for, that was for damn sure.

The last thing I wanted was for him to make a choice for *me* because I pressured him into making *my* dream come true. That was a sure path to resentment.

But... that didn't mean I couldn't figure out a way to show him just how good things could be if he stuck around, right? Before he left, I needed to give Charlie something to think about when he was back in Chicago. A reason to make sure he didn't stay gone for another fifteen years. A reminder of the true and solid things waiting for him in the Thicket when he was ready to claim them.

While I thought over this dilemma, Charlie's fingers continued to tease my skin, down my back and up my arms, until my mind lost its grip on my thoughts and I fell into a comfortable half sleep.

"I like you more than ever," I confessed from the safety of my drowsy haze. "I'm so glad you're back."

Another soft press of lips in my hair proceeded Charlie's murmur of agreement. "Not sure I want to leave," he admitted in a low voice.

As I drifted off to sleep, I thought I heard him add, "Not sure I can."

But in the end, I wasn't sure if the words were just another piece of my dream.

Chapter Thirteen

Charlton

WHEN I WOKE up the next morning, Hunter was gone. I found a note on the nightstand explaining he'd been required to chauffeur his mother and sister Black Friday shopping at o'dark thirty and would probably be out most of the day.

I blew out a disappointed breath. I'd hoped for a lazy morning with him, for more kisses and smiles, for more heartfelt conversations that might or might not be foreplay for something hotter... or, at the very least, would help me decide my future.

Instead, I pulled on my clothes, hopped in the side-by-side, and headed back to Amos's house for a Nutter family walk of shame. What was that old expression? Let no *nice* deed go unpunished?

But when I pulled open the side door and stepped into the kitchen, the place was surprisingly deserted. No raucous teasing cousins. No meddling aunts. Only my mom, Amos, and Emmaline remained, drinking coffee around the big table while discarded remnants of the newspaper took up most of the rest of the large wooden surface.

"Hey," I announced to the silent room. "Good morning."

All eyes swung toward me, and I tried very hard not to duck my head and blush like a person who'd snuck out in the dead of night for a private post-Thanksgiving rendezvous with a sexy local nursery owner.

I failed.

"Did you sleep well, Charlton?" Mom wondered. She looked me up and down with twinkling eyes. "You look *remarkably* well rested. I think the fresh Thicket air must be good for you."

"I did, thank you." I cleared my throat. "Where is everyone?"

"Up and out shopping since before sunrise, sweetie," Emmaline said. She stood and opened the cabinet. "But I saved you some breakfast. Sit down, and I'll make you a plate."

I slid into an empty seat between my mother and Uncle Amos, but despite the curiosity coming off them in waves, I avoided looking at either one. "So," I said brightly, nodding at the flyers. "What's on sale in the Thicket today? Any deals worth standing in line for?"

"Oh, plenty." Amos pulled one of the pages toward him and tapped his middle finger on it. "Two-for-one table saws over in Dooberville, so I sent Jaden and Jory to pick us up a couple. You need one?"

"Tempting," I said. "But I think I'm all set."

Emmaline handed me a plate of breakfast casserole, along with a perfectly doctored cup of coffee. "Down at the Wool You Be Mine, they're offering half off their entire stock of black yarn. But if you're interested, you best get over there before the Thicket Mourning Glories buy 'em out."

"The Thicket…?"

"Mourning Glories," Emmaline repeated with a wink as she took her seat. "You know, the local bereavement group?"

"Right. Of course." I darted a glance at my mom, who had pressed her lips together like she was trying not to laugh while pretending to be completely absorbed in her own sales flyer.

"You know, Emmaline, I think they'll probably make better use of the yarn than I could, but I appreciate the heads-up." I took a forkful of my breakfast and groaned. "This is amazing."

Emmaline blushed happily and turned back to perusing the flyers. A moment later, she gasped and covered the sheet with one hand. "Mercy!"

Amos glanced up. "What's that?" He grabbed the paper away from her. "Mpfh. Rite-Quick Pharmacy's running a sale on the ultra-mega pack of condoms. Good deal too. But I gotta say I'm glad we don't need those anymore." He dropped the page and turned to the sport section.

I continued to eat through the awkward silence, which, in hindsight, was a mistake. I should have taken the opportunity to change the subject.

"Although," Amos said, looking back up and tapping his chin thoughtfully. "I can ask your cousins to stop at the Rite-Quick for *you*, Junior."

I choked on my casserole. "Er… no, thanks, Amos," I croaked. "I'm good."

He narrowed his eyes at me. "You remember what I told you about bulls, right, son?"

"Yessir." I squirmed in my chair and added in a mutter, "Though I've tried hard to forget."

"And you know I weren't talkin' 'bout no *bulls* neither. That was what you might call a metaphor."

"I... yessir. I got that. I believe you were referring to particularly aggressive men."

My mother snorted her coffee.

Amos's cheek went pink. "Just so. Which is why you should think twice about passing up this deal, now that you're..." He looked at my mother, then waved his fingers at me in a vague gesture. *"Bein' nice* with that Jackson boy."

I shot my mother a look that said, plain as day, *This is your fault*, and she gave me a beatific smile in return.

"That there's another metaphor," Uncle Amos went on relentlessly. "For *sex*."

I buried my face in my hands. "Yes. I got it. Dear God," I mumbled between my fingers.

"I'm just sayin', love is love, kiddo, but there's no sense in anyone payin' full price for—"

"Can we stop talking about this?" I demanded. "Before I decide Black Friday shopping with the entire Nutter family would be a reprieve from the torture?"

Emmaline reached over and patted my hand. "There, there. Nothing embarrassing about safe sex... *especially* not when it involves that adorable Jackson boy. Did you know he once helped get a whole family of feral deer out of Monette Ivey's garden before they could eat her beloved heirloom romas? She insisted the boy deserved a medal for heroism... though I think, in the end, she just made him a nice platter of bruschetta."

My mom was having a field day with this. "Feral deer, you say? Are there others that are domesticated?"

Emmaline shot her a wink. "You know Monette has a way of embellishing a story. Wait'll you hear the one about the rabble-rousing groundhogs trying to start a coup in her zucchini patch. *'I tell you, they were* organized, *Emmaline. Someone put those groundhogs up to this!'* Next year, I expect the deer and the groundhogs will join forces, and no vegetable will be safe."

Mom couldn't hold back any longer. She laughed louder and harder than she had since... well, as long as I could remember.

"Only in the Thicket," she finally said, wiping a tear from her eye. "Gosh, I miss it sometimes."

"Well, that's easy enough to fix," Amos said. "Move on back."

"I've been thinking about that," she admitted.

I stared at her in shock. "You have? But... you couldn't wait to move away and start over. You used to make fun of the Thicket all the time."

Mom's smile faded. "Well, sure, but that doesn't mean I don't love it, honey. It's *because* I love it that I make fun of it."

I thought I understood what she meant. Hearing about all the Black Friday sales was amusing as hell, but where a couple of days before I would have been laughing *at* those things and the ridiculous town that spawned them, now I felt like I was in on the joke. Like my family's teasing, it was laughter born of affection and camaraderie... because in my heart, I belonged to the Thicket again.

But still.

"If you loved it, why'd you leave in the first place?" I demanded.

Amos and Emmaline exchanged a look. Amos lifted the paper in front of his face and pretended to be absorbed in the condom ad while Emmaline stood to clear the empty dishes and coffee cups.

My mom turned to me. "Back then, I needed things I couldn't find in the Thicket. A therapist, for one thing. A circle of other divorced moms who understood some of the challenges I faced, for another. But more than that, I think you and I both needed a fresh start. A chance to figure out who we were away from your dad's hometown... and his reputation. Your uncle Amos had helped us out so much for so long that I... I wanted to prove we could stand on our own two feet."

Amos reached over and grabbed her hand. His voice wobbled with emotion. "And you've done that a hundred times over. I'm so proud of y'all. But thank God you stayed in touch, Katie-Bird. We never stopped loving you as one of our own."

She squeezed his fingers tightly and turned her attention back to me. "I don't regret making that decision, Charlton. Not at all. But... just because a choice is right at one point of your life doesn't mean it's right forever. Just because you needed to leave doesn't mean you can't come home."

The thick lump in my throat made my voice sound hoarse. "Until this week, I didn't realize it'd still feel like home."

One corner of her mouth tipped up in a smile. "Maybe if you'd listened to me the past few years when I tried to convince you to visit, you'd have figured it out sooner."

My instinct was to argue, but then I remembered all the times she'd suggested I visit the Thicket for Christmas. "I thought you were suggesting it out of family obligation, not because you thought I'd actually like it enough to willingly stick around." I winced and shot Amos a guilty look. "No offense, Uncle Amos. Obviously, I love spending time with *you—*"

Amos snorted. "Can it, kiddo. You ain't so special. Plenty of folks get a wild hair to leave the Thicket. Why, when I was seventeen, I was so eager to leave I took myself down to the Army recruiter and signed up, just so I could get the hell away from your great-grandfather, controlling bastard that he was. Never made it past the testing, though, on account of my stammer was too severe."

Mom and I exchanged a confused look. "I've never known you to have a stammer, Amos," she said.

He shrugged. "'Cause I don't. It was cold as tits in the community center where they were doing the assessments, and I was shivering in my skivvies too much to explain without stuttering even more. But I kinda took it as a sign." He stroked his mustache thoughtfully. "Ya see, Jon-Carl Herbert decided to sign up on the same day, and that boy stank like a fish pond. If I'd gone along with my initial plan, I'da been stuck on a bus with him all the way to basic training. No, thank you."

I snorted. "And... do you ever wish it had worked out differently?"

His face lit up as he looked across the kitchen at his new-ish wife. "Not for one skinny minute. Not even in my 'what if' dreams. The life I've had here on this farm with these Nutters and all our friends has been the best life I could have imagined. Wasn't all perfect, o'course, and I couldn'ta planned for most of the things that happened, good or bad. Your father alone nearly put me into an early grave with his bull-pucky, and when your grandfather and his bride died way too young..." He shook his head sadly. "Felt like all the dreams we had for running this farm died with 'em. But that's how it goes sometimes. When the plan you had for your life goes wonky, you gotta come up with a new one. That's your privilege and your responsibility. Life's short; it's up to us to make the most of it."

"Hear, hear," Emmaline said, shuffling over to press a tender kiss to the top of his white head.

I took a shaky breath.

My mom reached out to rest her hand on mine. "Charlie, the reason I've been trying to get you back here, the reason I agreed to this whole niceness bet, was because I can tell you're not happy. You want stability in your life, and I get it. But, sweetie, stability doesn't mean working yourself into the ground while you cut yourself off from the people who love you. True stability comes from putting down deep roots that'll anchor you while surrounding yourself with people who'll nurture you into the strongest version of yourself and prop you up when storms come along. It means not being afraid all the time. And if you're starting to come to the same conclusions... maybe you're ready to come home."

My heart pounded unsteadily. Everything she was saying sounded *right*, but... I was afraid. It almost seemed too good to be true.

"Your mama's right," Amos said with a definitive dip of his chin. "If you were here, you and that Jackson boy could give things a real try—oh, don't you start telling me all the reasons you need to hold back or be cautious, Charlton Nutter," he said when I opened my mouth to argue. "Y'all care about each other—that was clear to everyone in town just by looking atcha, even when the pair of you were dancing around each other at the Stuffin'. When it comes to love, you two have enough pride and stubbornness for a whole flock of turkeys, but maybe the brains of *one* split between you. But that feelin' you got for each other? It's a gift. Don't second guess it."

"I... I..." My shoulders slumped. "I know it is. I've never felt this way about anyone before," I admitted. "But practically speaking, I can't just pack up and move. I have a job—"

"Mmm, and a job *offer* right here waiting for you." My

mother lifted one perfect eyebrow. "Buck told us about the offer he made you."

"I told him I was thinking of moving back here eventually, if I could make it work somehow," I admitted. "And he said he'd love for me to be in charge of logistics at his new company. Keep it all in the family. But Buck... he's not exactly reliable, is he? If the company failed, I'd be out of luck. And if it succeeded, I'd end up in a job that's just like the one I'm in now, doing way too much work with no personal involvement."

"Is that actually what he said, Charlton?" Emmaline's gently rebuking tone was so unexpected it cut deeper than any of Amos's bluster. "From what I heard, Buck wants *you* to decide what your position would look like. Said he'd even be willing to hire you as a part-time consultant if you wanted to work your current job remotely or find something else when you get here."

"Well." I swallowed. "He... he might have mentioned something to that effect, but I know how it would end up—"

"Do you?" she asked in that same tone. "Because Buck Nutter might be a rapscallion in a *lot* of ways, but he doesn't joke when it comes to his business. If he said it, he meant it."

I gnawed my lip as I considered this and let the possibility of having everything I wanted take hold in my mind.

"What did Hunter say?" my mother wondered. "Not that it's up to him, of course, but was he supportive of the idea when you told him?"

"I, uh..." I winced. "I told him I couldn't possibly consider it. He agreed."

Amos smacked his forehead with one thick palm. "I changed my mind. Callin' you two *turkeys* is an insult to the birds."

I thought of last night, when I'd told Hunter about Buck's offer. About the wide-eyed excitement that had flashed across his face before he'd tamped it down. My gut screamed that he felt some of the same things for me that I felt for him... so maybe it was time that I stopped being so scared and listened to it.

I needed to talk to Hunter. Again.

"We'll support you whatever you decide," my mother said gently. "What do you want to do, Charlie?"

"I want..." I began boldly. "...to go Black Friday shopping."

Mom's face fell, and she sighed.

Emmaline *tsked.*

Amos nodded disappointedly. "Decided the condoms were too good to pass up after all?"

"Not that kind of shopping." I stood and set my hand on the table. "Where do you think Alana and Lurleen would be hunting for deals right about now?"

The three of them exchanged a look. Chairs screeched as Mom and Amos shoved back from the table. Emmaline grabbed the keys to her minivan.

"Hot damn," Amos said, clapping his hands together. "Fetch my cane, Emmy! We going Hunter huntin'!"

"I'll text Lurleen right now and ask where to find them!" Mom said excitedly, already tapping on her phone.

"Noooo," I said, letting out the kind of laughter that comes with a sense of relief. I felt a strange weight falling off my shoulders and a new, tender but strong excitement taking its place. "No, no, no. We're not hunting anyone. I just need to pick up a few things for later. Hunter would *kill* me if I made some huge public declaration of affection in the middle of Socks n' More, especially before the two of us have had a chance to really talk about things. He hates being the center of gossip, and…" I shrugged. "He's important to me."

Emmaline clasped her hands—and keys—to her bosom. "Oh, sweetheart."

Amos pointed a thick finger at his wife. "None of those tears, now. We need your eagle eyes on the road. Let's go."

When we got to town, the crowds were worse than I imagined. Who knew Licking Thicket even held this many people?

"What the hell?" I muttered as we searched for a parking spot.

By the time we parked on Francis Street, made our way through the first of several stores I needed to visit, and clawed our way through the crowds to Walnut Street, all four of us felt like the walking wounded.

"What the hell are they selling at the Kinder-potamus store that's got everyone whipped into a frenzy?" I demanded, trying to catch my breath. "Some hot new toy the kids are asking Santa for?"

"No, they're after the tater tots," Emmaline said proudly. "Used to be that when you wanted to declare your affection for someone in the Thicket, you'd take 'em to the Steak n' Bait for tots. But then my grandson Jaybird started whittling some toy tots out of scrap lumber, and now they're all the rage with the young lovebirds in town. You get the same symbolism of abiding love and devotion you find in the regular shredded potato version, but these tots last forever."

I stopped and laughed out loud, right in the middle of the sidewalk.

How the hell had I lived without this town for as long as I had?

How fucking lucky was I that I got to have it back again?

"Junior," Mom said, clutching her cell phone tight, like she was afraid it might be lost and trampled in the crush, "I think we need to stop for a break now. Your uncle's trick hip is acting up." She grabbed Amos's elbow supportively.

"Oh, shoot. Uncle Amos, you should have said you weren't feeling well. But where can we stop?" I tried to peer over the sea of humanity. "Jesus. Literally every person in the Thicket must be out today. I don't see an empty bench anywhere."

"Naw, Junior, no need to stop on my account. I'm doin' just... *son of a biscuit!*" I turned back just as Amos's face crumpled and he began hopping on one foot. "I mean... yep, it's my hip alright. Sometimes the pain shoots all the way down my leg. Almost makes me feel like my toes are being stepped on," he complained.

"There's a pop-up cafe set up in a tent on the town square, and they're serving cocoa and cookies." Mom pointed. "Let's head there."

"You sure?" I stood on my toes and squinted. Even with my height, I couldn't get a clear view down the road. "I can't see the far side of the street, let alone the square. How do you know there's a tent?"

"Hmm? Oh." She waved a hand. "Who's to say? Must've read about it somewhere. You wanna talk about it some more, or should we move poor Amos along? Come on, Charlton." She pushed past me, leading Amos and Emmaline.

I blinked after her. "Jeez, someone's not even trying to win the bet anymore," I muttered, hurrying to catch up.

Sure enough, when we squeezed our way down Walnut Street to the square, there was a large white tent selling coffee and snacks. Folding tables and chairs formed an impromptu outdoor cafe with portable space heaters warming the area. Most of the area was already packed with Thicketeers exchanging intel on what kind of deals they'd gotten or exchanging bags of gifts to be hidden at each other's houses to foil pre-Christmas present-snoopers.

I gestured everyone toward an empty table under a heater at the edge of the tent and went to place our drink order. At the last minute, I added in some pumpkin-shaped cookies that looked good.

By the time I got back, our table was surrounded by chatty friends and family members... including Lurleen Jackson, who jumped up from her seat as soon as I arrived and tried to push me into it.

"Juni—*Charlie*," she beamed. "Don't you look terrific in that sweater? I love a man in cashmere. No, no, you sit here. *Right* here. I insist. I only ran over for a minute to say hello to your mother. I need to finish up my shopping and see where those children of mine have gone. How was your Thanksgiving, sweetie? I can't tell you how excited I was to hear from your mother that you were having such a..." Lurleen and my mother exchanged a mischievous look. "... *nice* holiday."

The two of them, along with Emmaline, collapsed into giggles, and even Amos snorted. I resisted rolling my eyes.

"It's been great, Mrs. Jackson," I said courteously, though I could feel my face getting warm in a way that had nothing to do with the space heaters. "Really... wonderful."

"Not as wonderful as it's gonna be," she said mysteriously.

I had no idea what she was talking about, and at that moment, I couldn't make myself care, even to be polite. As much as I loved being part of the town again, it was hard to relax and enjoy the festive atmosphere when so much was left unsettled between Hunter and me. I was impatient to get my errands done and get home. Heck, at this point, part of me wished Hunter would show up looking for his mother, just so I could pull him aside for a private moment to ground myself in our connection... though the rest of me was very glad he wasn't around to hear the teasing and feel the curious stares of the Thicket gossips.

I shoved an entire cookie in my mouth and took a big sip of my too-hot coffee to save myself from needing to make conversation, and as I chewed, I internally debated bringing up Amos's latest X-rated cow message.

Any diversion would be welcome, I decided.

And that was when I noticed the six-foot-tall turkey-man striding across the street.

A feathered headpiece and blue bow sat atop his cap of windblown brown hair, and a pink wattle nestled beneath a beard my fingertips had stroked only hours before. His colorful tail feathers bobbed in the wind as he walked confidently toward me, flanked by half the Jackson clan... and several highly amused Johnsons for good measure.

I spit my cookie all over the sidewalk.

Mom, Amos, Emmaline, Lurleen, and everyone else in the cafe area turned to see what had caught my eye. And as the turkey man got closer, I noticed the sign in his hands. The same sign I'd carried two days before.

Junior Nutter stole Hunter Jackson's turkey.

Only this time, the word *Junior* was crossed out with a big red line, and *Charlton* was written atop it.

And the word *turkey* had been crossed out and replaced with the word *heart*.

My jaw dropped, and my heart began to thunder. I glanced from the sign to his face. His jaw was firm and his shoulders set stubbornly as ever, but I could see anxiety in his eyes. I stood up and walked toward him. The grin on my face had to have been large enough to see from this distance.

"Hi," Hunter said, fidgeting with the sign. The entire town seemed to hold its breath while they watched the spectacle.

"Hey," I said softly.

"It, ah, occurred to me that I have some things I should probably tell you. So this morning, I got my mom on board, and she got your mom involved to get you here." His gaze bounced from me to our mothers, who were standing side by side, all four of their hands clasped tightly between them, watching us expectantly. "I figure, if you have two-thirds of the Thicket Matchmaking Mafia on speed dial, you might as well use them."

"You... arranged this?" I glanced at the crowd and added in a whisper, "In *public*?"

His eyes warmed and softened. "Did you think I just happened to be strolling around in this getup, baby?"

"I... I don't know," I said weakly. "I thought maybe I'd started a trend."

Hunter's brilliant grin would have stolen the breath from my body if I hadn't gone breathless the moment I saw him. "Maybe you have. Wouldn't be the only thing you changed when you came back to town."

Tears pricked behind my eyes. "Don't you dare make me cry, Hunter Jackson."

"Gonna try not to." He took a deep breath and grabbed my hand tightly in his. "When you went away fifteen years ago, Charlton Nutter, you took something incredibly precious to me. *Not*, as it turns out, my prize turkey—"

I clapped my free hand to my mouth to cover my snort-laugh.

"—but something way more important. You took...

yourself. Your kindness. Your intelligence. Your humor. Your friendship. And I understand why you had to leave. I even understand why you stayed away. I can't regret those years—they made you the man you are today, and I like that man too much to wish I could change a thing—but having you back made me realize just how much I've missed you. How much time I spent being angry with you when I should have simply *been* with you. How many jokes I've told without getting to hear you laugh at them. How many foolish things I've done without seeing you roll your eyes at me. How many times I've gone ice-skating without you falling on top of me. How many Thanksgivings have passed without you at my table. Hell, how many cups of coffee I've drunk without even knowing how you take yours—"

"With oat milk!" a voice in the crowd called.

Hunter's gaze flicked over my head for an instant. "Thank you, Savannah," he said solemnly. "That's helpful."

I laughed behind my hand again, but when Hunter's eyes turned back to me, he set down his sign and captured that hand too.

"I don't want to miss you anymore, Charlie Nutter. Not another day, not another *moment* that I don't have to. I want you back. In my life. In the Thicket. And I want everyone in the whole damn town to know it. I'll spell out JUNIOR COME BACK on Amos's cows if I have to—"

"Oh, honey, please don't," Joanie Brightly said from the crowd. "I beg you."

"God," I whispered, voice trembling. "Hunter, I—"

He squeezed my hand. "Now, I know you're probably not ready to move back here now. Maybe... maybe not even anytime soon. And I'm not generally a, uh, patient man—"

"Just ask anyone who's ever been in front of him at the

stop sign on Collins Road," my cousin Ollie agreed. "Man *lays* on the dang horn."

Hunter shot him a baleful look. "Jesus Christ. I'm trying to make a goddamn romantic gesture here, for fuck's sake, Ollie." He blew out a breath. "What I was saying was I'll try to be patient, Charlie. Because I don't want you to feel pressured. I don't want you to change your life around for me. I just want you to know this is what *I* want. *You* are what I want, and—"

I took one final step forward and grabbed his face before bringing my mouth to his and laughing into the kiss.

"You stole my heart, too, you turkey," I murmured against his warm lips. "I was coming over later to tell you I wanted to stay. If you'll let me... let me try to be a part of your life, that would be even better. I know it's quick, *too* quick, probably, but I'm done doing the cautious, stable thing when it means I don't get to be with the people I care about—"

It was Hunter's turn to interrupt with a kiss, this one with his arms—and feathers—wrapped tight around me and the sweet heat of his mouth so overwhelming it was nearly enough to drown out the reactions of the people around us.

"Wait, what'd Charlie say?" Uncle Amos demanded. "Turn up the volume, boy!"

"If he said no, he's letting my Hunter down *real* easy," Lurleen said exultantly. "You know, I think it was my reverse psychology that turned the tide."

"Are you kidding?" Alana demanded. "If I hadn't provided the turkey costume, none of this would've happened. Merry Christmas, Mom. You're welcome."

"*I* like to think it all started with our niceness bet," my mother sighed. "You can stop kissing him now, Charlton. You won, sweetie. The prize of your choice."

"How about making a nice big donation to the Castration Society in Charlie's name?" Emmaline suggested. "Castration is what brought them together, after all."

Hunter and I opened our eyes simultaneously in horror and began laughing too hard to kiss effectively, but that was no hardship. Standing in Hunter Jackson's embrace, laughing about the ridiculous town we loved, was almost —*almost*—as fun.

"So, why the costume?" I asked when we pulled back to grin at each other. "Not that I'm complaining," I added, taking in the sight of his muscular thighs encased in thin tights. "Not even a little."

Hunter shrugged. "I had you wear the costume to prove a point to the town, right? Only seemed right for me to wear it now."

I ran my hands through his messy hair. "Is it gonna be this way forever, then? Whenever one of us screws up, there's a turkey walk in our future to make amends?"

His lips widened in a satisfied grin. "Does this mean you plan on staying with me forever?"

Heat flooded my cheeks, but I was done hiding my feelings for Hunter Jackson once and for all. "I can't think of anything I'd like better," I told him and kissed him again... just because I could.

"Now, *that*," Lurleen said with a sniffle, "is the most majestic sight in all of Tennessee. Dolly Parton would be proud."

"Get a room, boys!" Amos shouted. Then, a second later, "No, wait, don't go anywhere yet. Emmy, run me over to the Rite-Quick. I need to see if that deal's still running."

"It's not too late," Hunter whispered roughly against my cheek. "Maybe we could both move to Chicago. Or New Zealand. Or the North Pole."

"Afraid not," I said mock-sadly. "Nutters belong in the Thicket, baby. And from now on, I'm not going anywhere."

Epilogue

Hunter

Christmastime - A Year Later

"I THOUGHT you were only here for nine pallets. You sure the manifest is correct?" I asked the semi driver as I kicked a clump of mud off my boot and watched it skitter over the gravel lot in front of our new plant warehouse.

The woman nodded, sending her thick gray ponytail swinging. "According to my information…" She looked down at the screen and frowned. "Wait. Maybe this isn't right after all. It says here it's a pickup arranged by a Charlton Heston Nutter. Somebody's pulling a prank on me."

I sighed and held back a smile. "Nah, that's right, then. He's my head of distribution and logistics. If he said we're sending eighteen pallets, we're sending eighteen pallets. Hang on, and let me get someone on the forklift. They'll bring everything out, and we'll get it loaded."

After catching Larry's eye and waving him over, I put him in charge of pulling the poinsettias out of the warehouse and helping me load them onto the truck. I watched with pride as the most gorgeous, pet-safe variation of poinsettias on the market wheeled their way from our warehouse to parts unknown. Now that Charlie had taken over distribution, our business reach had grown like kudzu vines in an abandoned lot. It seemed like Jackson's Organic Blooms were sold everywhere, and just this week Charlie had been out of town negotiating a new distribution deal with a company in Chicago to supply organic, pet-safe plants to several boutique stores in the metro area.

We were so busy Alana had called an emergency family meeting to beg our parents to make me stop using her event barn for overflow storage space between events.

My parents had agreed... and then invested the money needed to build a new warehouse right next to the one already half built with the company's own money. Now we had room to grow even bigger, and until the second warehouse was full, Charlie and I had a place to invite our friends over for impromptu roller derby parties.

It was working out fine.

When the dust from the departing semi finally began to fade, it was whipped up again by an unfamiliar gray SUV with a ride share logo placard in the front windshield.

Fucking *finally*.

I moved away from the warehouse door and toward the drive that led to the house, waving my ball cap in the air to get the vehicle to stop here instead of heading all the way up the drive.

Larry muttered, "He's been gone less than forty-eight hours, Hunt. Have some dignity."

I didn't take my eyes off the slowing vehicle as I replied. "No dignity needed, Lar. And don't make me remind you of the time Leela got back from her girls' weekend at Dollywood and you asked for a half day off to, and I quote, *get reacquainted with one another.*"

As Charlie pulled his overnight bag out of the car, I could hear him talking to the driver. "And be sure to stop at Wisteria Cafe on your way out of town—they donate half the profits from every coffee sold to the local schools, which really adds up. Tell Penny that Junior Nutter sent you."

"Thought your name was Charlie," the driver said in confusion.

Charlie shrugged. "Hometown nicknames have a way of sticking sometimes. You learn to get used to it. Drive safe, and thanks again!"

He turned to me just in time to catch me against his chest. I wrapped my arms around him and squeezed tight, inhaling the familiar, delicious scent of him, buried under the layer of airplane smell.

"God, I fucking missed you," I murmured into his neck. I took the opportunity to kiss and suck on it a little before nipping it hard enough to leave a mark. He yelped and pulled away.

"Fiend. Is that any way to treat the man who just closed tens of thousands of dollars in new business for you?"

I pulled back and stared. "They signed?"

He nodded proudly. "They did indeed. We owe Seamus a nice bottle of wine for introducing me to his old neighbor. I can't believe he was able to get me in with this group. But I'll tell you more about it after I change clothes. Oh, and maybe we can reheat one of the twelve Partridge family casseroles we stocked up on at the Stuffin' last week? I've been craving sausage for days."

"Behave." I smacked Charlie's ass just to hear him laugh.

I called over my shoulder to ask Larry to close up for me

before grabbing one of Charlie's bags in one hand and one of his hands in the other and starting the walk down the drive toward our house.

"Casserole's already thawing, thank you very much," I said smugly. "Musta read your mind."

"Musta had your own craving, more like," he said with a chuckle. "Before I forget, you have to help me figure out how to talk to Amos about the cow messages. It's getting out of control."

I groaned. "I'm guessing it didn't say LICKING THICKET CHRISTMAS FESTIVAL?"

"How about TICKLE FETISHES V THICK ARM? I don't mean to kink shame anyone, but..."

I smacked Charlie's... thick arm. "Just be glad we talked him out of using his cows to market our poinsettias because that would have been a phallic disaster."

"Speaking of the Christmas Festival... wait. Why doesn't it have a Licking Thicket name like the Wrappin' or the Carolin' or the... I dunno, Birthin'?"

"'Cause, baby..." I frowned at him seriously, trying hard to keep a straight face. "*Those* names would be silly."

He gaped at me for a long moment before realizing I was teasing, and then he hip-checked me nearly off the path. "One of these days, I'm going to stop falling for it, Hunter Jackson."

I laughed into the cold chill of encroaching dusk as our house appeared ahead of us through the trees and wrapped my arm securely around his waist. "I sincerely hope you *never* stop falling for me, Charlton Nutter."

Charlie let out a sigh and leaned his shoulder into mine as we continued to move forward together.

"Home sweet home," he murmured. "I fucking love this place."

As we climbed the porch steps to the front door, I marveled at how far we'd come in a year. It hadn't all been smooth sailing. In fact, it had taken Charlie so long to extricate himself from his job in Chicago I'd begun to think I was going to have to stage a rescue operation. But by Christmas, he'd been back in town, and by Valentine's Day, he'd been spending every night at my place. It wasn't until Memorial Day in May that he'd finally agreed to move in with me and stop pretending to live in the apartment above his cousin's garage.

He put down his bag in our entryway, pushed the door closed, and pulled me fully into his arms. The solid weight of him anchored me in every possible way.

"I started to ask you about the festival," he murmured against my chest. "We going?"

Pfft. Like this was an actual question.

Still, I pretended to think about it. "I dunno. Ava Siegel's newest kidlet is playing baby Jesus in the live nativity. Last year, the town *lost* the baby Jesus—thankfully, played by Wattle, Diesel and Parrish's turkey—for a full forty-five minutes when he wandered off during a set change, which makes the use of a real live baby a smidge risky, despite Ava's assurances that there are plenty more Siegels where that one came from. My mother says there will never be another baby so well protected in all their lives, but it sounds to me like that's code for every busybody in the Thicket showing up to be ready when the drama begins."

"Can't wait." He leaned in and kissed my neck in all my favorite places. "What else did I miss while I was gone?"

"It's only been two days," I said with a grin, enjoying every minute of his tongue's attention.

"Longest two days of my life."

I began unbuttoning his jacket. "Oh, you missed Red Johnson changing the town population sign by one."

Charlie lifted his head up. "Oh yeah. Who moved in?"

"My friend Lane. You knew that."

He leaned in to kiss the base of my throat. "He's been here six months already."

"But the sign doesn't change until there is a signed lease or an official real estate transaction of some kind."

Charlie snorted, soft, warm air blowing into my neck. "Jaybird Proud needs to start requiring paperwork even if he's not going to charge rent."

I peeled off his jacket and flung it in the general direction of the hooks behind the door. It landed in a puddle on the floor. Next was his shirt. I yanked it out of his pants and ran my hands under it along his hot skin.

"Now that it's official," I said, "Lurleen, Cindy Ann, and Katie-Bird have decided poor Dr. Lane needs a man."

Charlie stopped what he was doing and threw his head back, howling with laughter. "Oh my God, that's the best thing I've heard all week. The Matchmaking Mafia has Lane in their sights? Good. Then they can lay off us for a while."

It took me a minute for his words to sink through my lusty haze, but then they landed with a thunk. "Oh. You don't want to... oh."

He looked at me funny, but before he could ask me about it or before I could ask him if his harmless comment actually implied he wasn't in a hurry to take the next step in our relationship, the doorbell rang.

I squeezed my eyes closed in frustration. "It's probably Larry thinking it would be real funny to interrupt our homecoming. Give me a minute."

I opened the door, fully prepared to yell at or possibly

fire one of my best employees, when I saw Diesel and Parrish Partridge standing on the front porch with an animal carrier in one hand.

Diesel beamed. Parrish looked a little less sure.

"Uh, hey, guys," I began, turning to look at Charlie in case he knew the reason for our evening visitors.

"Ah, shit. I lost track of time. Sorry." He nudged me out of the way and grabbed the carrier. "Thanks, Diesel. I owe you one. A big one."

He grinned at Diesel, and Diesel grinned back. Parrish and I looked at each other, and then Parrish caught a glimpse of Charlie's untucked shirt and the marks I'd left on his neck. He grabbed his husband's elbow. "We should go, babe."

Diesel frowned. "We should stay."

"Nooo, we should *definitely* go," Parrish insisted.

"You should go," Charlie said politely.

Diesel frowned. "But I would really like to stay."

Charlie scowled at Diesel, muttered an apology to Parrish, and then slammed the door in their faces before turning to me. "Hunter... you know I love you, right?"

I looked between the man of my dreams and the pet carrier uncertainly. "Baby... Butterbean's not that old," I began. "But she's old enough not to want another dog around. We haven't even *talked* about getting a puppy—"

"It's not a puppy." Charlie's eyes held a soft understanding. "And if you decide you're not interested in having another animal, you won't hurt my feelings in the slightest. Diesel said he can take it back, which probably means keeping it himself."

The sound of the Partridges' truck driving away faded, and Charlie opened the front door to peek out. "They're gone. Come outside."

I followed him outside, where he sat me on the top porch step and asked me to wait. *Patiently*. The reminder of my promises in the town square made me roll my eyes... but otherwise, I didn't move a muscle. I knew I would always wait for Charlton Nutter... just like I knew he'd always come back to me.

When he returned a few minutes later, he was dressed in one of his oldest, softest cashmere sweaters—one I'd told him many times last winter was my favorite—and a clean pair of blue jeans. He rubbed his hands on his thighs before taking a deep breath...

And I decided right then and there that whatever animal was in that box, poisonous or venomous or anything in between, we would keep it. Anything Charlie wanted that badly, I wanted too.

I opened my mouth to tell him so.

And that was when he got down on one knee.

I stared at him. The air in my lungs shrunk, and my heart skittered to a stop. "Ch-charlie?" I breathed. "Are you... is this...?"

"Baby." He blew out a breath and opened the pet carrier before reaching in and pulling out a tiny, ugly-as-sin turkey chick. "Meet Tammy Wynette."

"I don't understand," I whispered. Except I did. I was almost positive I did. And that knowledge did not one single thing to make my breath come easier.

"Hunter Jackson. Love of my life. My partner in crime. Will you accept this little poult as a symbol of our new beginning, our love and our forgiveness, our challenges and our triumphs, our efforts to nurture and grow not only each other but ourselves and our business as well? Will you join your life with mine permanently? Will you... will you marry me?"

I closed my eyes just long enough to thank the universe for landing me in this town with these people and this crazy life.

Then I opened my eyes and said... *yes.*

———

Want more Licking Thicket romance? Check out more hilarious reads set in the punniest small-town in America...
Flakes (Colin and Ryder)
Fakers (Brooks and Mal)
Liars (Diesel and Parrish)
Fools (Dunn and Tucker)
Peacocks (Lane and Jay's story)

Letter from Lucy & May

Dear Reader,

Thank you so much for reading *Turkeys*! If this is your first book by one of us and you'd like to read more, we suggest you start with *Fakers*, book one in the Licking Thicket series, or Lucy's *Borrowing Blue* and May's *The Date*.

We would love it if you would take a few minutes to review *Turkeys* on Amazon, GoodReads, or BookBub. Reader reviews really do make a difference and we appreciate every single one of them.

We've been friends and fans of each other's work for a couple of years, so we weren't surprised when writing our first collaboration went so smoothly. We were surprised, however, that it didn't end up being a standalone novel like we planned. The town of Licking Thicket stole our hearts and now we've turned a standalone into a series! Check out the complete Licking Thicket series on Amazon, including

the final book, *Peacocks*, which is now available here →
https://readerlinks.com/l/4488351

Our most recent cowritten series is set in another delightful
small town and you can go here → https://readerlinks.com/
l/3077980 to check out all the shenanigans in
Honeybridge, Maine. And if you like to stay in the Thicket
a little longer, check out our spin-off series, Champion
Security → https://readerlinks.com/l/4189908

Be sure to follow both of us on your favorite retailer site to
be notified of new releases, and look for us on Facebook for
sneak peeks of upcoming stories. You can also join both of
us on Patreon for exclusive content and behind-the-scenes
glimpses. Find Lucy here → https://readerlinks.com/l/
4255454 and May here → https://readerlinks.com/l/
4255455!

Feel free to sign up for our newsletters, stop by www.Lucy-
Lennox.com, www.MayArcher.com, or visit Lucy's Lair
and Club May on Facebook to stay in touch.

To see fun inspiration photos for this book, check out the
Pinterest page for Turkeys.
Happy reading!
Lucy & May

More From Lucy and May

Licking Thicket

Flakes

Fakers

Liars

Fools

Turkeys

Peacocks

Champion Security

Hijacked

Hitched

Hacked

Honeybridge

Firecracker

Mr. Important

About Lucy Lennox

Lucy Lennox is the USA Today bestselling author of over fifty gay romance titles including the GoodReads Hall of Fame winner Wilde Love. Born and raised in the southeast USA, she is finally putting good use to that English Lit degree she earned before the turn of the century.

Lucy enjoys naps, pizza, and procrastinating. She stays up way too late each night reading romance because it's simply the best.

For more information and to stay updated about future releases, sales and audio news and to grab some free and bonus reads, please sign up for Lucy's author newsletter on her website at LucyLennox.com or to stay in the know, join her exciting reader group, Lucy's Lair on Facebook.

facebook.com/lucylennoxmm

instagram.com/lucylennoxmm

amazon.com/Lucy-Lennox/e/Bo1No1OYPT

bookbub.com/authors/lucy-lennox

patreon.com/lucylennox

pinterest.com/lucy_lennox

Also by Lucy Lennox

Find me online → https://linktr.ee/LucyLennox

Read my books:

Made Marian Series

Forever Wilde Series

Aster Valley Series

The Billionaire Brotherhood Series

After Oscar Series (with Molly Maddox)

Twist of Fate Series (with Sloane Kennedy)

Licking Thicket Series (with May Archer)

Champion Security Series (with May Archer)

Honeybridge Series (with May Archer)

Find a complete list of my stand alone romances and novellas at www.LucyLennox.com along with audio samples, freebies, suggested reading order, and more!

About May Archer

May is an M/M author who lives in Boston. She spends her days planning vacations, mainlining diet soda, avoiding the gym, reading M/M romance, and when all other forms of procrastination fail, writing it.

Visit her website at mayarcher.com to sign up for her newsletter to hear about sales and upcoming releases, freebies and behind the scenes info and more! Or join her Facebook group, Club May!

facebook.com/may.archer.author

instagram.com/mayarcherauthor

amazon.com/May-Archer/e/B075JQVGLX

patreon.com/MayArcherRomance

bookbub.com/authors/may-archer

Also by May Archer

Find me online → https://linktr.ee/mayarcherauthor

Love in O'Leary Series

Whispering Key Series

The Sunday Brothers Series

Copper County Series

The Way Home Series

Licking Thicket Series

(cowritten with Lucy Lennox)

Champion Security Series

(cowritten with Lucy Lennox)

Honeybridge Series

(cowritten with Lucy Lennox)

For a comprehensive list of titles, audio samples, freebies, suggested reading order, and more, visit my website at www. MayArcher.com!